# ALLOTMENT PLOTS

A ROUND OF SEVEN DEADLY

ARABLE PARABLES

# Peter Skyte

The right of Peter Skyte to be identified as the author of this work has been asserted by him in accordance with the Copyright, Designs and Patent Act 1988.

All rights reserved. No part of this publication may be reproduced, stored in a retrieval system, or transmitted, in any form or by any form or by any means without the prior written permission of the author.

This is a work of fiction. All of the characters, organisations and events portrayed in this publication are either products of the author's imagination or are used fictitiously.

Copyright © Peter Skyte

## CHARACTERS

Stacey Portslade

Hugo Wivelsfield

Bill Southwick

Daphne Littlehampton

Joan Riddlesdown

Nigel Hassocks

Clive Portslade

## Stacey's cucumber

It was a cucumber that had been her nemesis, she would later think. Who would have thought that nearly twenty years of married life would be compromised by a vegetable? Or is a cucumber a fruit? But then vegetables – or fruit - are the staple of allotment life, and allotment activities had formed an increasingly dominant part of Stacey's early middle-aged life.

In her twenties, and becoming established in a successful modelling career, she found it easy to entice a succession of eager suitors, attracted to her growing fame and easy glamour, notably her startling green eyes and stunning shoulder length blonde hair. If truth were told, not that she would ever afford herself the luxury of being honest with the truth, she had also put herself about quite freely. Glorying in the head-turning attention she attracted on the arm of her latest beau at every celebrity and fashion event, Stacey had become ever needier to move on to her next conquest. And there had been many. She knew she used men; there was a compulsive lust from a within her that she did not understand. A lust from somewhere, something, some time, to exploit, to dominate, and to control. Yes, she had to control.

Then she had met Clive. Perhaps she had tired with constantly burning the candle at both ends and the continual whirligig of paramours she would later think. She was getting increasingly bored with the self-centred, egotistical and in truth empty headed men she seemed to attract. Clive was different, so different. Attractive in his own way, comfortable in his own skin, and palpably intelligent, he was also kind, generous, and a successful well-connected lawyer. For once, she saw in him the potential for a long-term relationship and someone with whom she could settle down – as her mother had urged – and start a family.

After a whirlwind romance she and Clive had married and the succession of one and very occasionally two-night stands had ceased. They had settled down to a suburban life of comfort and domesticity; he a lawyer in a well-regarded if somewhat mundane high-street practice, she continuing with lower key modelling assignments.

With the entry into their life of first a son and then two years later a daughter, Stacey had given up work to look after the children. She had thrown herself into parenthood and watched their two children move progressively from childhood through adolescence to late teens. As she entered her early forties and the demands of parenting gradually diminished with the maturing of the children, Stacey began to nurture a growing resentment at the sacrifices she had made, and the recognition and attention she had forgone.

They had acquired an allotment more to keep in with the practices of some of their social circle rather than as a conscious interest in cultivating crops. Having taken on the responsibility they both felt an obligation to at least make the effort to engage with their newly acquired plot. Stacey channelled her energies increasingly into the seasonal activities required to sustain a broad range of crops, notably cucumber plants. Clive's initial enthusiasm for the courgettes they had planted in of the raised beds had waned, as had the plants, and he now appeared to spend more and more time in the office, or so he told her, only helping out occasionally at weekends.

And then Hugo Wivelsfield entered her life, in every sense. It had started as a casual encounter at the allotment, when Clive had been present for once, and Hugo had made a rather lewd remark about the courgettes. She had noticed Hugo sporadically, as he worked on the nearby plot. Although she had initially paid him little attention, she was aware that the same could not be said for him. Unerringly, Stacey always seemed to know when she attracted the attention of a man. She sensed he had been staring at her, when her back was turned, and had taken the time to dress in a manner she knew would attract his approval.

Late one afternoon, a few days later, she found herself weeding at the end of her patch. A deep rich voice, revealing an undoubted private school upbringing, abruptly interrupted her day dreaming.

"Your cucumbers, they really are rather splendid and so huge."

She looked up and rather startlingly found herself gazing directly into the deep brown eyes of the man from the neighbouring plot. Although she had of course noticed him at a distance, she had not seen him close up before, nor exchanged anything more than a peremptory nod and a polite 'good morning' or 'good afternoon' as the exigency of the day required. He was tall, probably forty-ish she guessed, well built, surprisingly well dressed for allotment work in a loose-fitting powder blue shirt and navy chinos, and clearly bore the manner of someone supremely comfortable in their own skin.

"Thank you. I'm in to big cucumbers," she had responded unerringly, vaguely conscious of an echo from a long gone past and her first encounter with the man who became her husband.

Her words produced a guffaw, which was quickly suppressed, and all of a sudden she realised the implications of the double-entendre she had inadvertently uttered. She could feel a deep blush spreading, and out of nowhere she burst out laughing. Hugo followed suit, and they both laughed uncontrollably for a good minute at least. When they had both composed themselves, introductions followed. Hugo had a free and easy manner and before long the initial brief exchanges had developed in to a deeper conversation.

Stacey glanced at her watch, not so much out of the need to rein in the free-flowing conversation, more a desire to see how long they had been chatting.

"I'm so sorry, I must be keeping you," Hugo said, noticing the downward flick of her eyes.

"No not at all. Actually, my husband is meeting a client and won't be back till late," she found herself saying, surprising herself by the openness with which she volunteered the information.

"In that case, why don't I invite you to come back for a glass of wine," Hugo responded. "Although I say it myself, I am something of a fine wine connoisseur. We allotment neighbours should get to know each another and I live close-by."

Although vaguely aware of the potential implications, it had been so long since anyone had taken such an interest in her that Stacey had taken up the offer after a momentary hesitation. Hugo lived in a small cottage-like house some ten minutes' walk from the allotments. He had told Stacey within the first few minutes of their conversation at the allotment that he lived on his own, and the house bore all the hallmarks of a solitary male household. Not only was there an absence of homely trappings and trimmings - a few pictures dotted around the otherwise bare walls, empty windowsills and no indoor plants to be seen – the kitchen sink and work surfaces were covered with the detritus of more than one day's meals.

Hugo did appear to know a lot about wine, not that she would have known if he was talking complete gibberish, and poured her a lavish glass of white wine. "Obviously it's a white, but which country and grape?" he enquired.

"I don't know… I don't know much about wine," she answered.

"Go on, at least have a guess."

"French?" she replied, mentioning the first country that came into her head.

"Mmm, not quite right. Grape?"

"Chardonnay?" the only grape she could recall.

"Game attempt, but actually it's a South African Chenin Blanc, 2022. Fresh but nicely rounded on the palate, don't you think. Anyway, cheers. First of the day".

"Cheers."

"Bottoms up!" he rather overenthusiastically proposed, and burst out laughing. He had an infectious laugh, and unable to help herself, she followed suit. Although the toast was in many ways a perfectly straightforward expression of a certain type, fashioned by class and age, she suspected a deeper meaning. Their eyes locked, with the force of two magnetic poles irresistibly drawn together.

Although he was obviously flirting with her, she found the full-on attention extremely flattering. It had been such a long time since she had enjoyed the company of a man clearly bent on chatting her up. She felt a stirring deep within her of something long suppressed, and felt a returning desire to flirt outrageously as she had in the past.

"You've given me a large one".

The words burst out, before she could stop herself, not that she would have wanted to. They both burst out in unrestrained laughter again. Two hours later, and a little giddy after a few more glasses, how many she could not remember, she rose to her feet.

"I really must go", she said, realising that this was the second or third time she had promised this.

"Such a shame. We were just getting to know each other. We must do this again."

"We must" she heard herself saying.

"See you at the allotment. A bientôt", Hugo said, as he gripped her shoulders and planting a kiss on each of her by now flushed cheeks.

Momentarily she leant into him, wishing he would go further, but then she recovered her composure and departed. In the ten minutes it took for her to walk a little unsteadily to her home, her head a fuzzy swirl and her body an emotional whirl, she felt the stirring of a lust long suffused. The yearning to overwhelm a man again.

She was already in bed, her mind in a whirl about Hugo, when Clive returned home. He perfunctorily explained he had been caught up in some complex litigation matter, not that she took any of it in, and after a superficial peck on her lips, he wandered off to the ensuite to pursue the time-consuming rituals of his nightly ablutions.

Next morning, after Clive had left for the office, she hurried down to the allotment, eager to see Hugo. He was not there, and disappointed she scratched around her plot, without doing anything very productive. A few minutes later, she heard a whistling and looking up, saw Hugo walking purposively towards her.

"Hello" came the rich basso profundo voice. "What a lovely morning. And all the more lovely for seeing you."

"About last night. I...I..."

"…I know" he interceded, "We shouldn't have stopped so soon. We should have carried on, it was just getting interesting."

"I..we..no... yes" she stammered, turning away, unsure of herself but also keen for him to say more. Much more.

"Well, better get on with some weeding," he remarked, and walked away to the ramshackle shed which stood, or rather leaned unsteadily like a drunk in need of support, on the far side of his allotment plot.

How offhand, she thought to herself. She went through the motions again of looking busy, trying to appear to be fully engaged in allotment activity, but her mind was elsewhere. Very elsewhere. She pottered around for a couple of hours, desperately hoping that Hugo would come over, but he seemed more interested in talking to another allotment holder, Bill Southwick, the elderly man who chaired the committee which ran the allotments. Two can play that game, she thought, and went over to where Joan Riddlesdown was busily tending to her rhubarb.

"Hello Joan, Fancy some lunch?" Stacey asked. "It's been a long and hard morning."

Joan readily agreed and they went off to the 'Original Oak', one of the local pubs. No doubt there would once upon a time have been a distinguished oak tree, perhaps even original, but any trace had long since vanished. After a rather tired Caesar salad that she picked over, Stacey returned to the allotments eager to see if her avoidance strategy had rekindled his interest, but Hugo was nowhere to be seen.

For the remainder of the day and all that evening, she was totally consumed by thoughts about Hugo. It was mad, she tried to tell herself, but her heart refused point blank to respond to her head. She barely knew him. How much time had they spent together? A couple of hours at most, but she was engulfed by a desire for him. No, it was more than a simple desire. A fire burned within her, her chest felt tight, her lips were dry. She lusted after him. She wanted him, She had to have him. She would have him.

The next day, there was no sight or sound of Hugo. Nor the next day. The following day, as she was bent head down pinching out some tomato plants in mid-afternoon, she felt a presence behind her. Standing up, she turned round and there was a grinning Hugo.

"Been avoiding me, have you?" he brazenly enquired. She felt the heat of an angry rejoinder welling in her, but her eyes met his and her resistance melted.

"Seeing as you ask, I have been tending to my cucumbers", she smiled. "They needed some attention otherwise they would have flopped", she added coquettishly, feeling emboldened and gazing unswervingly into his eyes. How his eyes, deep and brown, smiled and twinkled.

"I can't imagine any cucumber going soft in your hands", Hugo responded, with an all too unashamed wink. She felt herself starting to blush, but then recovered her composure. This was a game she had played many times – and what seemed like many years – before. She had form and experience in the finer arts of male enticement. And she wanted him, God how she wanted him. "It looks as if it is going to rain" she said, gazing at the sky. "How about continuing your course of wine appreciation?"

"Great idea", he responded unhesitatingly. "Let's go back to my place".

Together they left the allotments, walking the short distance back to his house. They exchanged not a single word. She hungered for him to make contact, tense with anticipation of what was surely to follow, but he kept his distance until they were in his house with the front door closed. Once inside and away from any possible prying eyes, they fell on each other. One form of abandonment was followed by another wilder form of abandonment. Hell, it felt good. She gorged on their physicality. Much later, with an interlude for a glass of some fizzy white wine, they uncoiled and rolled apart, their passion sated.

"I must go home. Clive will be coming back and I must freshen up before he arrives" Stacey murmured into Hugo's ear. She dressed with her back to him, knowing that if she turned to look at him, she would not be able to tear herself away. Fully clothed, she had the confidence now to face Hugo, who was lying with his hands interlocked behind his head, staring vacantly she thought at the ceiling. "See you at the allotment" she rather weakly said, departing without so much as a farewell kiss or hug.

Clive returned at around eight o'clock that evening, and they ate a meal of pasta and salad, discussing somewhat mechanically the deeds of their day, or in her case not quite all of the deeds. Later in bed with Clive asleep and gently snoring, Stacey found it difficult to get to drift off, her mind a tumult of swirling thoughts and emotions; an element of guilt certainly but also a feeling of justification. Well, their marriage had become a humdrum existence from day to day and week to week, trapped in a rut of monotonous normality. Hugo offered a jolt to the equilibrium, which she readily seized.

The following weeks, the affair blossomed. They would meet at his house – she felt that being together in her house at that stage would be an act of defilement, for reasons she could not really fathom. On the allotment, they would work at their adjacent plots, stealing yearning glances from time to time, before retiring to his place. Retiring? Hardly an appropriate description, she thought, as they ever more voraciously devoured each other.

She learned more about Hugo's background, as she lay close to him, embraced by his strong and muscularly arms. His upbringing, attendance at one of the older universities, expulsion for drug excess, early success followed by a hushed-up dismissal for insider dealing in his City trading days, and latterly working from home as a commodity trader dealing in something or other in a world she didn't really understand.

Although they had tried to carry on a pretence of mere acquaintance at the allotment, she knew that suspicions were mounting amongst some of the other allotment holders. That interfering know-all, Daphne Littlehampton, had made some sarcastic comment about how it was encouraging to see allotment holders getting on so well. Her friend, Joan, at one of their occasional lunches at the pub, had enquired about whether Hugo was sharing some special expertise as they seemed so often to be engaged in deep discussion. Stacey wasn't sure if this remark was made from complete and utter innocence or something else. Not that she cared, or so she told herself.

But there began to develop a gnawing qualm. Although Clive's visits to the allotment had become rarer, she wondered if an idle comment by one of her fellow allotment holders – most likely from that busybody Daphne – might alert him to her transgressions.

And then some months later, there had been that ghastly business at the allotment AGM. All over a pumpkin. Would you believe it, what drab petty lives must some people lead? That Bill guy, from somewhere up north, a true missionary, miscreant…she struggled for the word. Misanthrope, yes that was it, one of those words she remembered her father using, but never really knew what it meant. She still didn't, but it sounded good in her head.

Ah yes, her father. She suddenly felt sick, and tried to expunge the memories, but it was too late. Clive knew a little about the way she had been treated by her father, but not the complete history and the real truth. No-one did, other than her; certainly not her mother. It was too painful and traumatic. Although on the odd occasion since her teenage years she had felt a compulsion to let someone in to the dark secret she harboured, she had resisted, fearing the resultant raw emotions that would flood forth from something deeply buried within her. She had once – no twice – been on the verge of seeing a psychotherapist, but had buckled at the last minute. The second occasion had been in the practice waiting room, where she had crumpled, made an excuse, and rushed out, not to return.

The tryst with Hugo she did not regard as an affair. That was too formal, too organised, and implied a degree of commitment, or at least mutuality of obligation, of which she felt none. It was nothing more than a sensual lust to be desired and to devour and be devoured physically. It was merely an arrangement, although a convenient one. This arrangement could not go on indefinitely, that she knew. They had become rather carefree about taking precautions to escape direct observation as far as they could, but the oblique and sometimes more direct references by Daphne whatever-her-name continued.

After nearly a year, they had also become more relaxed about the length of time they spent together in bed, on the floor, on the sofa, in the bath, and in a variety of internal and occasionally external locations. On a couple of occasions, she had rushed home without showering to find Clive already home. Although aware that her flushed state and lingering pheromones might raise some suspicion, she had enough confidence to provide what appeared to her to be a suitable covering explanation of her whereabouts and activities that day. Or so it seemed, and Clive had never sought to question or challenge her. Not only did he seem to display little interest in what she said she had been up to, after the initial information he was positively disinterested.

Of late, Hugo had increasingly pressed her to make love in her house, in her bed. She had firmly turned this down, not because she hadn't wanted to experience the risky thrill but by rejecting his entreaties, she knew she exerted control over his craving. She had to be in control, and to exercise power over him.

Just as power and control had been exercised over her during her childhood all those years ago. It would happen, but only when she decided.

One day, as he helped her lift a large piece of dead vegetation, after she had teased him mercilessly about the pumpkin affair and his attempt to laugh it off, she considered that the moment was opportune. "Thanks for your help and effort. I couldn't do without you," she pouted, putting on her most seductive throaty voice, and lowering her eyelids as she stared deep into his eyes. "Why don't we go back to my place for a change?"

Hugo looked startled for a moment, and then recovered his composure, smiling. "Are you making a statement or posing a question?" he responded.

"Take me in any way you want," she whispered flirtatiously.

"Do you realise, I don't actually know where you live?"

"Then I suggest you follow me home, but keep a discrete distance."

They walked to her place, him trailing behind her. Stacey walked as slowly as she dared, in the full knowledge that this would increase his desire for her. Once back in her house, she led him upstairs to her bedroom, pushed him backwards on to her bed and sat astride him. For the next couple of hours, they romped and rolled with an intensity like nothing before, glorying in the delights of each other's bodies.

It had been a novel experience in more than one sense, as they had playfully teased each other about early sexual encounters. She had not been entirely open with the truth when recounting teenage experiences. What was that phrase from the 80's or some such? Economical with the truth. Yes that was it, she had been economical with the truth. She omitted to mention the treatment she had received from her father. Disclosure had its limits after all. Hugo's totally unexpected revelation had so stunned her that they had got up rather later than she had intended. Dusk had come as they untangled their limbs from each other, showered and went downstairs.

"You had better go now. Clive will be home soon". Stacey passionately kissed Hugo as they stood by her front door. They were so engrossed with each other that neither heard the crunch of footsteps on the gravel path outside, and it was not until there was the unmistakable sound of a key turning in the lock of the front door that they awakened to their imminent plight. But it was far too late, as Clive entered, stopped abruptly, and stared at the all too obvious evidence before his eyes.

"What's going on?" he asked, completely unnecessarily, in a strange tone of voice she thought. "I think you had better leave" he said to Hugo, surprisingly calmly, she thought in the circumstances.

After Hugo had mumbled something and departed swiftly, Stacey blurted out "It's..it's…not what you think…", certain in the knowledge that it was exactly what he thought, with good reason.

"You think I hadn't been aware of what has been going on with that man? I think we had better sit down in the lounge and talk", and with that he turned his back on her and walked towards the door into the lounge.

Stacey followed him and sat down, nervous yet curious as to why he had seemed so calm and resigned, and waited expectantly for what he was going to say to her. Whatever it was, it could hardly be as dramatic as Clive catching Hugo at her house. Ironic, as it was the one and only time he had been there. Did Clive really know what she was up to with Hugo for all the time he had claimed, or was it merely a lawyer's bluff?

But it transpired that what Clive had to say was even more dramatic. Utterly unexpected and a complete bombshell she would never forget.

**Hugo's pumpkin**

"Your pumpkin was a reet champion".

Hugo heard an unmistakeable gruff Yorkshire voice emitting from the other side of the makeshift fence that separated their allotment plots.

"Best in class by a mile at the End of Season show. It well deserved to win the cup."

"Yes, it was rather special", Hugo said, not really wanting to make conversation. "I only decided at the last minute to enter it for the competition."

"Strange one, mind," said Bill, "It's a surprise that no-one remarked on it before the day of the show. You must have kept it under a fig-leaf or summat."

"Yes, it was a surprise to me as well, emerged out from under." Hugo responded, annoyed at the need to continue the conversation, although he knew a response was necessary to allay any suspicion.

"Beginners' luck. But no match for the splendour of your cabbages. Now must get back to my labours, such as they are."

****************

Hugo was a relative newcomer to the allotment community. He had rented his allotment for around 18 months, which was a mere blink of an eye by comparison with some of the other long-standing holders. Bill Southwick claimed to have been tending his allotment plot for over 20 years, essentially full time since the death of his wife a few years ago.

Hugo's thoughts went back to the End of Season event, the occasion when the best products of each allotment holder were displayed in the large hut, and each member would proudly reveal the produce of their season's till and toil. He smiled inwardly to himself. Little did any of them suspect the provenance of his pumpkin, which had indeed won the prize for Best in Class.

How had he managed to end up like this, alone and surrounded by a motley assortment of tiresome allotment holders? An allotment? How had it come to this? Had he betrayed the expectations, the fortunes of circumstance as much as wealth, that his upbringing had surely intended of him? Still there had of late proved to be more than adequate reward for the drudgery of horticultural routine.

****************

Peyton Hugo Erroll Wivelsfield. Quite a mouthful. Two names derived from grandparents and the last from his paternal great grandfather, a little known baronet and landowner. At the minor Catholic public school he had attended in the north of England, his sobriquet had been Phew, from the initial letter of each of his names. His intense dislike for Peyton had led him to use the second of his names from his mid-teenage years, once he felt sufficient confidence to cast off the burden of his parental naming. Not that confidence had ever been much of a hindrance to his character. The one blemish in his existence had been the misfortune to be a second born, and it was his elder brother who would succeed to the family title.

His schooling had been fairly typical of his background and generation, moderately but lazily academic, and enlivened by discovery of the joys of illicit drugs and first sexual escapades with maidens from a nearby girl's school. Much to the disappointment of his parents and the school, he had failed to get a place at Oxford or Cambridge, his undoing being a sexual caper on the night before the vital exam which had interrupted his preparation and concentration.

His university experience at Bristol had revolved around girls and drugs, or sometimes drugs and girls, until some quite needless drug dealing had resulted in his expulsion. Why he had felt any necessity to deal in drugs when he could exist financially very comfortably on the monthly parental allowance he would ponder from time to time in an idle moment. Somehow sufficiency was never enough. He was greedy for ever more.

Through connections of his father, Hugo had secured a job at one of the City's lower profile investment banks, just at the time when anything went as long as it made money and prior knowledge was deniable by superiors. He had revelled in an environment where the principle of greed was regarded as a virtue, and his natural greed drove him to increasingly risky investments and trades which provided a quick healthy return, as long as everything went smoothly.

Two marriages had come and gone. The first to the daughter of his then boss had ended as a result of his involvement with the woman who led to the second. Neither had lasted long enough to result in any children. Not that he had any real desire to surrender to fatherhood, despite the coaxing and pleading of his mother, who was desperate to have grandchildren. He satisfied his desires through a number of affairs, usually with younger women who could be seduced by his arresting looks, effortless charm and easy way with words. Life had its compensations and long lasting relationships whether in business or pleasure were not his thing.

And then suddenly one week, everything in the business failed to go smoothly and his losses had mounted up. For once he was no longer able to cover up through risky gambles and his – and more importantly the company's – financial exposure had been discovered. His undoubtedly unlawful activities had been quietly and efficiently hushed up at the cost of his job, not that the quiescent City regulator was overkeen to expose anything which could crawl out from under financial stones and stall the motor that powered the country's overinflated economic bubble. Big bang had led to big bucks. He was 'let go' to pursue an alternative venture, as it was described. No-one was ever openly sacked or dismissed at that time in the City.

Hugo sold his well-appointed Docklands flat, which had greatly appreciated in value since the purchase with one of his grotesquely inflated annual bonuses, and moved to a small terraced house in the commuter belt. Using some money his father had yet again provided to bail him out, he had set up a commodity trading business, operating online from home. He had reined in, at least for most of the time, his previous recklessness and greed for vast riches and settled down to more modest but still appreciable returns on his trades and investments.

Women had been of late strangely absent from his life. He was, he mused to himself in a rare moment of introspection, a semi-feral being, only partially domesticated and possessing wild instincts which were subdued rather than curbed. At least he had an allotment, which he had put his name down for in another moment of self-absorption. He had thought that allotment activity might help him to lay down some roots in the local community, as well as in the soil, but he had largely failed to succeed with either. Quick wins with the minimum of effort were his driving forces, and that mindset rested uneasily with the patience and input required to nurture crops and communality.

It had been a full year, for all sorts of reasons, not least since he had started his liaison with Stacey. His first sight of her bending over while tending to some crop or other on her allotment plot, had aroused his interest. He had leant on his fork, watching her golden blond hair shimmer in the soft sunlight of a spring morning. As she uncoiled from her bending position to stand erect, he had watched spellbound as she tossed her hair back and delicately wiped her face with a hitherto concealed white handkerchief withdrawn from some place on her person. What a figure.

Although hardly the most appropriate attire for allotment activity, her close fitting emerald green blouse and denim blue jeans tightly stretched over her posterior displayed her physical attributes to full effect. He felt a greed for her, a reviving of the force that had always driven his late thirty something years of life, and that all too often been his nemesis.

Hugo had initially pursued Stacey with some caution. He had not summoned up his ready confidence to even engage in any flirtatious banter with her, let alone a conversation. At the time, he had mused that he must be slipping up. Eventually late one afternoon after a modestly rewarding day's trading from his home office, his mind made up, he crossed the grassy path between their respective plots, his greed to seduce another woman unleashed. So began their affair, which had overwhelmed him for the best part of a year so far. What a woman. His insatiable greed and her unquenchable lust conjoining in physical congress. Without question the best lay he had ever known.

\*\*\*\*\*\*\*\*\*\*\*\*\*\*\*

Hugo awoke from his daydream with a start.

"I said how did you manage to grow such a fine specimen?", Bill's gruff voice with the flat northern vowels nearly deafening him. "I've never had a pumpkin like that in all my years on this allotment."

"Ah you know Bill, beginners' luck", he responded, his thoughts returning to the present.

If only they knew the real secret of his success, although he wondered whether his encounter with that dreadful Daphne woman at the supermarket in the build-up to Halloween might have raised some doubts in her mind about the provenance of his crop. She really was an interfering busybody; just his luck to run into her. With Bill Southwick, he had established an uneasy relationship, relying on him for advice and tips on tending to his various crops, although Hugo had steered clear of any mention of pumpkins.

"Will tha be at allotment AGM do next week?" Bill enquired. "It's important for holders to support t'Committee and let us know what you think."

"Yes I expect so", Hugo replied. "Must show willing, and all that."

"Champion. See you there", and with that, Bill shuffled off back to his own plot, the creak of his boots at each step bringing to mind a scene from those horror films where an inn sign swings squeakily in the wind, immediately prior to some ghastly event.

"Silly old sod," he said under his breath, or so he hoped.

Hugo spent much of the next week working at home, making money from buying and selling commodities with the mere click of a keyboard. He turned up at the allotment a couple of times, more to see Stacey than to carry out anything other than the most token task on his plot. On both occasions, they were soon back at his house, dining on their desire.

Come the night of the allotment association Annual General Meeting, Hugo had snuck in and sat at the back of the community hall. He spotted Stacey sitting attentively near the front, but hoped that no-one had observed him stare at her divine form. His attention drifted as the meeting bore on, in every sense he thought. Long winded speeches, and tedious bureaucratic items of business. Who cared whether the allotment association had a Membership Secretary, or a Tools Allocation Officer. Certainly that afternoon Stacey had no need for such a functionary. God, she was a great fuck.

His revelry about the day's earlier activities was suddenly interrupted by the sound of his name being spoken. He looked up, and saw that the infernal Daphne Littlehampton was on her feet to his left.

"That Hugo Wivelsfield," she vented, pointing at him. "I saw him at the supermarket, buying a pumpkin. The one supposedly from his allotment that won the End of Season class wasn't grown by him at all. It's a fraud and so is he."

Everyone in the hall turned round to look at him, and he felt his face flush. Through all the visages of shock and anger, he caught sight of Stacey who gave him a pronounced wink, which he desperately hoped would not be noticed by anyone else. He saw Bill Southwick, who was chairing the meeting, get to his feet.

"Na then, Daphne. Hold your horses for a moment. Let's hear what t'laddie has to say for himself."

"Yes, what do you have to say for yourself?" he heard the loud nasal-rasping voice of Nigel Hassocks.

In a daze, Hugo heard a low rumble of murmuring from the other allotment holders, still turned towards him, glaring daggers. He was about to own up to his folly, when he thought better of it. Nuts to them, this is an allotment association, not the City of London

Fraud Squad. He decided to brazen it out, and stood up to face Bill at the top table.

"Nonsense", he declaimed forcefully. "She's got it all wrong. I was examining the pumpkins at the supermarket, but only to compare their weight and texture to those I have grown myself."

He paused, pondering whether to stop there or wade in to Daphne Littlehampton and her revolting kind. His mind made up, he plunged on and in. "If Mrs Littlehampton", he continued, putting on his most condescending tone of voice "had bothered to ask me what I was doing, I would have told her and saved us all from this farrago of innuendo and insinuation. If she had a life of her own, and desisted from her constant meddling and stirring, perhaps she would do us all a favour. She's an interfering busybody with nothing better to do with her time."

"Now, now laddie", he heard Bill say from the front of the room, "Let's keep this civil. I know you are summat of a newcomer and have not been on the allotment as long as some, and don't put in as much time as the rest of us, but we are all friends here. That last remark was uncalled for and quite unnecessary."

Hugo was on the verge of responding, fuming with indignation at the patronising language of the chairman of the allotment association, when to his surprise he saw Stacey rise to her feet, a few rows of seats in front of him.

"I'm sure that Daphne simply made a mistake. Easily done. Let's move on", she said, clearly attempting to smooth over the incident.

"She's hand in glove with him, assuming, that is, her hand isn't somewhere else on his anatomy" he heard a female voice mutter disdainfully from somewhere to his left, followed by barely suppressed titters from a few of the allotment members present.

Hugo couldn't hold back his feelings any longer. "Daphne, you're a crabby old goat", he yelled, ploughing on and unable to restrain himself. "Why if I were married to you, I would end up poisoning your tea"

To his complete surprise, she responded with her own insult. "And if I were married to you, I would drink it," she retorted." You are nothing but an obsessively self-centred scoundrel, lowering the tone of our neighbourhood."

An eruption of laughter followed this salvo, incensing Hugo even more.

"And as for the rest of you, you are all a bunch of losers."

With that, he gathered up his jacket from the back of his chair and stormed out through the door at the rear of the hall, leaving the ensuing uproar behind him. He hoped that Stacey would follow him out, but there was no sign of her as he headed home.

Time passed, and he returned to scratching around on his allotment. Bill what's-his-name came up to him one day and asked him to apologise to Daphne Littlehampton, but he had declined to do so unless she apologised to him for casting aspersions about his pumpkins and other matters. None of the other allotment holders referred to or mentioned the kerfuffle at the AGM, and Daphne Littlehampton studiously ignored him.

The afternoon routine with Stacey carried on two or three times a week. It therefore came as something of a jolt to this established routine of their trysts when Stacey suggested completely out of the blue that they went back to her place one afternoon. They had always gone back to his house, and despite his pressing her on a number of occasions, she had adamantly refused to entertain the notion of a liaison at hers. Quite understandable really, he knew, but he was greedy to conquer forbidden terrain, scale the final peak, the triumph of their togetherness as he saw it.

Perhaps it was the sheer unexpectedness of the event, and emboldened by the attainment of his aspiration, he dropped the guard he had mounted over all those years. He had told Stacey before about much of his life story, about the two failed marriages, and the City escapades culminating in his being 'let go'. He had tried to explain his current trading ventures and what was involved, but she was either unable to comprehend or disinterested in his endeavours, most probably both.

Luxuriating in the aftermath of their physical pleasure, they had goaded each other to reveal details of early sexual adventures. They had exchanged cursory outlines on the when and where but not much on the who. Hugo had, consistent with the braggadocio of his gender and the swagger of his persona, naturally exaggerated the scale and frequency of his successes in response to her insistent teasing.

Stacey referred to early teen experimentations with what he considered a rather calculated elusiveness, her inscrutability impossible to pierce. He was surprised, although not altogether astounded, by the number of her liaisons, which Stacey seemed to regard as conquests for some inexplicable reason. Well, the world of modelling provided such opportunities and probably expectations in order to get on.

Abruptly out of nowhere she flirtatiously whispered into his ear. "How old was the youngest one you ever shagged?"

Caught unawares, his mind still immersed in the love play, he answered without hesitation. "Fifteen. She was a real stunner, advanced for her age"

"Well we all went through early teenage experimentation with sex", she replied.

"No, it was much later than that". Too late, he realised the folly of his remark. The predictable follow up question ensued.

"Oh. How old were you then?"

He froze, his body tense with anxiety as to where this conversation was heading. He was unable to complete the remaining and anticipated detail.

"How old" she repeated, separating her body from his.

"It doesn't matter," he muttered weakly, knowing that this would not put an end to what was now an inquisition.

"I said, how old were you when this took place?" she probed, insistently.

"Umm….well…it…twen…thir…thirties. Thirty five, actually" he stammered.

"Thirty five?" she exhaled, raising herself to rest on her elbow and staring bewitchingly at him. "Did anything happen? You know, were there any…"

"...consequences?" He finished the sentence for her. "Nah, not really. I paid her off."

"You old devil."

Her head bent forward and inserting her tongue into his ear, she licked him lasciviously. He felt her long fingernails beginning a slow journey down his lower abdomen, but their remorseless descent was interrupted by her sudden shriek. "Oh my God! Have you seen the time? You must go. Clive will be home any time now."

With that, they had both jumped out of bed, hurriedly dressed and rushed downstairs. But they had been too late, and Clive had entered the house as they were in the middle of a passionate farewell kiss, the touch and taste of her lips transmitting a tremor down his spine. Christ, that women could kiss like no other.

Later that night, after coming home feeling as if he had a tail between his legs, he ordered a curry to be delivered and hit the bottle of blue label Scotch he had stored at the back of his drinks' cabinet. The spirit had been a gift from a business acquaintance for some long-forgotten favour. He had been saving it for a special occasion, but this was the occasion to throttle it, special or not.

His thoughts returned to the earlier events of the evening. Was this the end of the arrangement with Stacey, he wondered? What would she be thinking and doing? Had her husband given her a hard time? Was Clive the type that would resort to physical violence with Stacey or more worryingly himself? His mind was a mass – no, more like a mess - of conflicting questions and an absence of answers.

He took another slug of whisky, the liquid producing a warm burn in his throat as it passed through on its way through his alimentary system. He cast his mind back over the course of his life. How had he ended up like this. Running a small business on his own, with no-one to share the post-adrenalin rush of successful deals after hours in City wine bars. The exclusive club he had been barred from, with no reason given, although soon after he left the finance company, was there a connection? No-one at home to await his return and dinner on the table. His elder brother replete with family, title and mansion.

A memory stirred, penetrating the increasing bitterness and churning of his emotions. The recollection of the recent AGM of the allotment society, and the way he had been singled out. That Daphne woman. A dragon. And that Bill, the chair, or chairman as he adamantly insisted on. What a patronising and pompous northern oaf. A rising anger engulfed him. The humiliation he had suffered, in front of everybody. He desperately wanted to exact revenge on his tormenters.

Yet another slug. The anger subsided, the rudiments of a plan forming. All of a sudden, he knew. He would show them. He would teach them a lesson they would not forget in a hurry. How dare they besmirch his reputation? Had he been both sober and capable of self-reflection, of which he was neither, he might have deliberated that he had little reputation to besmirch. His mind made up, he got up, lurching unsteadily to the door.

He grabbed his gardening jumper from the peg, opened the door and went out into the cool night. A reddish moon was high in the sky as he headed for the allotments. He unlocked the metal gate to the allotments, stumbled through more by luck than judgement, and pressed on.

Through his alcoholic haze and the evening darkness, he spotted a flickering light through the window of a shed on one of the plots, and headed towards it.

## Bill's cabbages

The cabbages had been a labour of love over the many years that Bill had tended his allotment, particularly so since the death of his beloved wife Brenda three years ago. They were his pride and joy, and he would talk endlessly about them to anyone who he could collar in the Flounder and Ferret any and every evening.

Bill had been born and brought up in the small Yorkshire mill town of Ossett. No-one outside the old West Riding had heard of the place, and he had become accustomed to having to conduct a lesson in geography, to anyone who enquired as to his place of birth, describing it as a town near to Leeds, midway between Wakefield and Dewsbury. He had left school at fifteen, which was the norm in those days and those parts.

After an apprenticeship in the local shock absorber factory, long since closed, he had entered the army at the tail end of National Service, serving in Kenya during the Mau Mau revolt. Despite waxing lyrical about his past, the Kenya Emergency was the one part of his life he would resolutely never discuss with anyone. He knew why. He was of that generation where you didn't talk about military experiences and with good reason. The flashbacks and nightmares of what he had witnessed and endured told him why.

Most of his working life had been spent as a fitter at an engineering plant. Back then the factory had a post-entry closed shop and trade union membership was a condition of employment. On his first day, the role of the union was explained as part of his induction process. He had been active in the union, joining the shop stewards' committee and eventually succeeding to the position of convenor.

He had met Brenda at the Mecca dance hall in Leeds, presided over at that time by a disc jockey with long blonde hair and an absurd sense of dress and decorum. They had courted for two years and then married. Two sons followed, but they had grown up and left the family home to lead their own lives some years ago. Bill and Brenda developed an interest in ballroom dancing which was their customary Saturday evening activity, until her knee joints began to give up on her.

When the factory closed in the late 1990's, Bill had been made redundant along with the rest of the workforce. They had sold their house and coupled with his redundancy money bought a small flat in the suburban south east, near to where their elder son and his family now lived. Bill had secured a plot at the nearby allotment and had devoted much of the last twenty years to growing various crops, of which the cabbages were his pride and joy.

Over the years he had developed an affinity with nature's seasonal rhythms, of which the various cabbage varieties provided a substantial source of evidence. He grew Kilaton for winter and Gunma for summer cropping, and could wax lyrical for hours about the specific characteristics of each.

In point of fact, he could pontificate about most aspects of allotment life, which he did most of the time to anyone who would listen. Now that he no longer had Brenda to share his views with, he regarded himself as the wise elder statesman of the allotment. He was the sage amongst the sage, as some wit had once described him, and he sported the accolade with deep pride. As chairman – stubbornly resisting the designation of chair - of the allotment association from as far back as anyone could remember, he bore the weight of his office with the requisite responsibility demanded of the calling.

"Morning Joan", he called out as he threaded his way around the allotment plots on his tour of duty. "I see that Hugo bloke has failed to tidy up the path by his patch yet again. What are we going to do with him?"

"Yes he doesn't really seem that committed", Joan replied.

"And he didn't take part in the work weekend neither. What a scamp."

"Maybe he has been up to other things", said Joan, with merely a hint of something in her manner that caused him to pause his passage.

"He's certainly up that Stacey Portslade for one," came the cackling sound of Daphne Littlehampton as she emerged from the shed on her plot. "She's as bad, the pouting slut. Her poor husband. I've a good mind to tell him what that pair are getting up to behind his back."

"Now now, Daphne," admonished Joan. "We are all adults fully capable of living our own lives without interfering in those of others. By the way, how's the dog?"

"My little dear's not been too well recently, "Daphne replied. "His diet has been upset. It's difficult at this time of year."

"Daphne, it's hardly surprising." Bill said, rather gruffly. "If you insist on only feeding vegetables t'little blighter."

"Well he is very partial to my offerings, and it's good for the environment", Daphne answered, somewhat haughtily. "I am trying to be green."

"T'little blighter were certainly green when I last saw him", he guffawed. "So was his vomit. All over Nigel's garlic… probably the best feed they have had for some time mind".

"Do you think we ought to do something about that Hugo," said Joan, intervening in an attempt to return the discussion to safer ground. "He's a freeloader and it's really not right that he doesn't do his share of communal activity."

"That man's a frightful disgrace," opined Daphne. "Lowers the tone of the neighbourhood. Can't we do something about him?"

"Like what," asked Joan.

"Expel him from the allotment association. Kick him out," barked Daphne, in a manner not to be contradicted.

Bill pondered for a moment, conscious of the weight of his responsibility as chairman of the association. He also found it a bit rich for Daphne Littlehampton to complain about disreputable behaviour, given her record. "Well t'working weekends are only voluntary, and we have no means of enforcing action on the paths…"

"…unbelievable. What a bunch of spineless wimps you lot are," said Daphne, interrupting him, her face doing its best to imitate a Les Dawson mother-in-law impression. "Surely the Council Allotments Officer can do something."

Bill momentarily tossed round in his mind whether his notion of hell was to be trapped on a desert island with either Hugo Wivelsfield or Daphne Littlehampton as his sole companion. Ugh, what a prospect. Which was the lesser of the two evils? He rescued himself from the dilemma of having to make a choice between the irksome and the fearsome by contemplating that there was an even more terrifying possibility. He could be stuck with both of them together. Hell is other people, as someone once wrote.

With a sense of relief, he was conscious of hearing his voice replace his wandering mind. "Let's think this through. We are overdue in carrying out our committee allotment inspection. His allotment is an overgrown and untended mess, if you ask me. We could do a dirty plot inspection, give him a warning and fine him. If t'bugger doesn't tidy it up, we could if t'committee agrees contact t'authorities to take away his plot. It would need a formal motion to be carried with a two-thirds majority, mind."

"Ooh, that would be a trifle drastic" said Joan, clearly surprised by the severity of his statement.

"Not before time, I say." said Daphne. "Would serve the cad right. Should cut his nuts off at the same time. He has the purity of a putrefying pineapple."

Bill suppressed a laugh, as he contemplated the image, but Joan was unable to stifle her giggles.

"You do paint the most graphic image, but I've not seen pineapples on these allotments recently? Dear me, Daphne, you do go on about him. Give it a rest," she managed to say after regaining control of her fit.

"Well, I'll talk quietly to rest of t'committee," Bill responded. "Now must get back to my cabbages, the beauties."

He turned and wandered off to his own plot. He had his own views of why Daphne Littlehampton was unable to resist constant digs at Stacey Portslade and Hugo Wivelsfield, and their off the field activities, knowing a little about Daphne's life story, and how she had been left high and dry, deserted by her wealthy husband just before Christmas one year. Daphne had never remarried, and as far as he was aware, had never had another relationship since her divorce.

It was hardly a great insight to understand that she could be exceedingly jealous of Stacey and Hugo. Although Bill himself had not looked seriously at another woman since the death of his wife, he could appreciate Stacey's striking allure, which even her gardening garb could not mask or conceal, and Hugo's undeniable appeal to the fairer sex.

Despite his episodic aversion to Daphne Littlehampton, with her ludicrous airs and graces which did not sit comfortably with his background, a bond had developed between them. She had been supportive of him and his role in chairing the allotment association, and helpfully loyal in some sticky times at allotment meetings. He was one of the few who knew that she customarily had a bottle of sherry to hand in the lean-to shed on her plot, and occasionally he would be invited to have a glass.

"Hello me lovelies." Bill cooed to his cabbages, to which he devoted copious care and attention. Since the death of his beloved wife Brenda three years back, the cabbages had taken her place in his affections. How he loved them, and they reciprocated, providing him with so much pride and joy. Cabbages did not answer back, argue or backbite about other people; not something that could be said about some of his fellow allotment holders. He liked talking to the cabbages, not that they had much to say in return, now that he no longer could talk to Brenda.

Apart from Joan, and occasionally Daphne when a sherry was proffered, he had few others he could open up to about his feelings. Small talk with some of the other members about allotment activities was fine up to a point, but he never felt comfortable in expressing his personal feelings and frustrations to people who to him were emotional strangers. Most definitely, he had never mentioned to anyone the circumstances of Brenda's passing.

Like many men of his age and generation, the pub afforded a degree of solace. In his younger days, he had usually gone for a drink after a union meeting, but since the early days of starting their family and in Brenda's lifetime, pub visits had dried up. He mulled the words over in his mind as he contemplated this description of his activity, or rather lack of it. Curious turn of phrase he thought, drying up of pub visits. Hmm. Now that he had little to keep him at home in the evenings, he habitually wandered down to the Flounder and Ferret, and the coterie of regulars he mixed with there. On occasion he would meet up with Joan for a drink, usually after a stint on the allotment.

Allotment activities consumed much of his daily routine. It was not just the horticultural tasks of tending to the cabbages and other crops, but the officerial responsibility of chairing the allotment association and wider role as allotment elder statesman. He took to the part like a duck to water, or on further reflection perhaps more pertinently like a hoe to untilled soil. It came naturally, given his background as union convenor for so long. He used to describe his convenor role as akin to herding cats, and that referred just to the other shop stewards, never mind the members he represented.

The Personnel Manager at the engineering plant had once said to him in a private moment that he saw Bill as a potential supervisor, possessing as union convenor many of the strengths and skills required in management. At that time, Bill was uncertain about whether the Personnel Manager was casting a bait to see if he bit, or merely offering a passing comment. Whichever it was, he never followed it up.

As he worked on his allotment ground, Bill would from time-to-time brood about whether in chairing the allotment association he had finally arrived at his managerial position, or was simply continuing his convenor role.

Whatever it was, the skills he had built up over those years needed to be deployed to resolve the petty spats and squabbles which seemed to arise with wearisome regularity between some of the allotment members. Whilst the cast list varied, the highest probability was that one or more of Daphne Littlehampton, Nigel Hassocks or Hugo Wivelsfield would be among the protagonists and antagonists. Still, every allotment has its tiffs and petty quarrels he had been advised by the Allotments Officer, it was just that theirs had more than its fair share.

Prior to the recent AGM, Bill had felt a sense of unease, some foreboding of events yet to unfold. He knew that the committee elections would be largely a formality; no-one was likely to challenge his position as Chairman, although he had for a couple of years anticipated that someone, possibly that nit-picking Nigel, might seek to burnish their equal opportunity credentials by proposing that this position be retitled as Chair, but to date that challenge had not arisen. Nor would Joan Riddlesdown be challenged for the Administrative Secretary position; there was too much time and effort required – largely unrecognised and certainly unrewarded - for anyone to want to carry out this role.

There was a certain status, and most definitely petty power, in the position of Facilities and Resources Officer, but Nigel Hassocks had done a good job for the most part, even if he was prone to take advantage of the office for his own benefit. Anyway, who would challenge Nigel? Hugo – definitely not. Daphne – too much hassle for her, plus it would remove one of the targets of her whingeing. There was the potential for someone to raise other hardy perennials, such as the lack of water pressure when certain members hogged one of the taps, or one of Nigel's foibles, but he would know how to deal with those. His factory floor experience had prepared him for such eventualities, and he took pride in his ability to maintain order and conduct AGM business.

And then it happened. He was caught completely on the hop at the association AGM, taken aback by the accusations levelled out of the blue about Hugo Wivelsfield by Daphne Littlehampton. Bill himself had praised Hugo's pumpkin, but never thought anything more of it. He had done his best, or so he thought, to lower the temperature when feelings ran high, but he had in all likelihood failed in his efforts.

Daphne had been right out of order. Why hadn't she mentioned her concerns with him, so he could have a quiet word? Quite understandably, Hugo Wivelsfield had been angered by Daphne's questioning of the provenance of his pumpkins, but that could be no excuse for the manner in which Hugo had reacted. Bill had tried to calm down the tumult which followed, but it took his considerable skills to eventually bring the AGM back to order.

Fortunately Hugo had stormed out, otherwise the uproar would have lasted far longer. He had approached Hugo at the allotment a few days afterwards in an effort to persuade him to make peace with Daphne, but Hugo had abruptly brushed him aside and insisted on an apology.

Some further days later, he entered the allotment ground rather later than usual in the afternoon, after a visit to his doctor, to see a group of the members standing round his plot, visibly in an agitated state. Daphne was remonstrating with Stacey. Nigel was involved in an animated exchange with Joan, his hands flailing wildly in all directions, and another member whose name he could never remember was crouched on his knees. As she caught sight of him, Daphne ceased whatever she was bickering about and stomped towards him in her green Hunter wellingtons.

"Bill! Bill! Have you seen what he's done? This time he has gone too far," she exploded.

"Who? Wha...wha...what are you talking about," he stammered.

"Have you seen what he's done to your plot?" Daphne shouted.

Bill had now reached the first of his raised beds, and his gaze alighted on a scene of utter carnage. The cabbages, in which he took such pride and delight, had been entirely uprooted, torn to shreds and scattered far and wide over the bed and the adjacent grassy path. Most of his other vegetables had been pulled out and hacked to pieces. He was stunned, and stopped dead in his tracks. He felt tears welling up in his eyes, and his hand went to his forehead.

"My cabbages, my beauties. How could anyone do this to you," he howled, sinking to his knees.

"And that's not all. He has destroyed my daffodils," wailed Daphne, her words ending in a shriek.

Bill stood up and Daphne quite unprecedently put her arms around him to console him. He sobbed uncontrollably into her ample chest.

"What am I to do? All that work in vain. How could anyone do this?" He wiped the tears from his eyes and blew his nose.

"He's gone too far this time. He's got to go," Daphne screeched in his ear.

"Who? Who are you talking about?"

"That Wivelsfield man. Hugo of course. That scoundrel. It's obviously him, getting his own back after what happened at the AGM," she said, beginning to calm down.

"Quite right. It has to be him," came the unmistakable rasping voice of Nigel Hassocks.

"Look, we don't know for certain it was Hugo," said Bill, releasing himself from Daphne's consoling embrace. He wiped his eyes with the back of his hand, slowly regaining some of his fabled composure. All his experience as union convenor in dealing with the unexpected kicked in. "We mustn't jump to conclusions."

"Well who else other than Hugo would have done this deed. It's an outrage." Daphne resumed her rant at full throttle, almost directly into Bill's ear canal.

"Trust me, I'm a detective, it's him", intoned Nigel, in a manner that denied any possibility of contradiction. " I passed him late last night slinking away. He looked very shifty. I always knew he was not to be trusted, that public school arsehole. If only I had caught him in the act, I could have cuffed him there and then."

"Do you have to use such vulgar language," Joan added, rather more firmly than was usual in her case.

"Cuffed, it's a policing term."

"No, not that," Joan replied, "the other word."

Daphne quite unexpectedly grabbed Bill by the hand. "Why don't we go over to my plot, and have a sit down by my shed. We need a shot of something to calm us both down." And with that she led him away.

They sat down on the ramshackle bench beside her shed, barely strong enough to support one rather than the two of them. "Now, I'll get us both a small libation," she pronounced. He was in no state or position to refuse. As she stood up, the bench seat quivered and creaked as if in gratitude for the lightening of its load.

The top half of Daphne's torso disappeared into the shed, her not inconsiderable derriere protruding out into the afternoon. "There we are," she said, returning to the seat and proffering him a grubby plastic beaker filled almost to the brim with an oaky coloured liquid. "Chin chin." She clinked his glass, or as approximate to a clink as could be generated with the actual vessels in hand.

Their initial exchanges over what to do about Hugo's future as a member of the allotment association soon morphed effortlessly into more general chinwag. Daphne gossiped about several of the other association members; he, more circumspect, but gradually loosening his tongue as the periodic replenishment of his beaker took hold. He knew a bit about her background, and she added to his sum of knowledge about how her husband had left her for a gameshow hostess from some satellite TV channel he had never heard of.

'All fur and no knickers' was Daphne's contemptuously dismissive description of the replacement in her husband's affections, her bitterness all too apparent. As the afternoon wore on and the sherry flowed down, Bill's sight of her face blurred and all he could focus on was the movement of her mouth, her ruby-red lips separated by her tannin-stained teeth shifting up and down and from side to side as the torrent of words gushed endlessly. Daphne's husband had been a multi-millionaire property developer who had moved on from early shillings and pence entrepreneurial dealings, buying and selling foreign stamps in the school playground, to substantially richer pickings.

She mentioned several Russian sounding names as if he should be instantly familiar with whichever oligarch she made reference to. Evidently they had been household names in her household he mused, but quite definitely not in his. The one item of detail fascinating to him was the financial arrangements of the divorce, and Daphne's enduring resentment of the terms of the settlement. For reasons he could not fathom, the experience had led Daphne to become a vegetarian.

As the light began to fade, and feeling a modicum of embarrassment at the direction of their conversation, if that could be used to describe an endless, one-way stream of wrath, Bill intervened at one of the sporadic interludes when Daphne paused for breath. Undoubtedly the quantity of sherry consumed had something to do with it, but completely to his own disbelief he found himself talking about Brenda. No doubt the destruction of his treasured cabbages which had taken her place had been a factor in stirring him out of his reticence. For the first time since her death, he found himself opening up about their life together, and to little more than an allotment acquaintance at that. He had never spoken to anyone, not least his children, even though Harry lived in the vicinity.

Perhaps It was a need to provide a distinctive contrast to Daphne's scathing contempt for her ex-husband and his belle – it was a toss-up he thought as to which of the two produced the more eviscerating scorn from her – that unlocked his emotions, gave rise to a feeling of devout tenderness and prompted him to talk about his bereavement.

"Well, tha sees, she was t'first and t'only love of my life," he explained, following the recounting of their courtship and early life together. "We were married for over 50 years. I could not imagine life without her, and that she would pass away before me. It were a nervous condition, tha' knows."

"Nervous? Why was she nervous? Was it about money?"

"Not nervous in that sense. An illness of the nervous system."

"Oh, a neurological condition, you mean," she said.

"Yes, that was it. I'm not very good with long words or talking about it. It makes me so sad, that I just want to cry. But us men isn't supposed to do things like that."

"You poor thing," said Daphne, the usual stridency of her voice reduced to a mere whisper. "What you must have gone through."

"Yes, it went on for nigh on three year."

"My my," Daphne murmured, resting her hand gently on his arm.

"Towards the end, she were not able to feed herself. I had to feed her and wash her. Like she used to do with the kids when they were young. I had a bit of help, but it were the nights that were most difficult." He stopped, willing himself to hold back the impending tears.

"Bill, I understand. You don't need to say anything more."

Something buried within him caused him to press on. "That's not all. There's summat else…" he mumbled, his voice almost inaudible.

"What else?" Daphne responded, unable to restrain her curiosity and desire for him to finish whatever he had embarked upon.

He paused, momentarily regaining some composure. "It were so difficult for her during her last three months. She was in so much pain and discomfort, just lying there unable to speak or move."

"I'm sure you did everything you could to care for her. I really feel for you."

"I just had to help her. It's what she wanted."

"What did she want?"

He paused, staring ahead into the distance. "I just had to do it. There was now't else to do."

"Do what?"

"Bring an end to her misery and suffering."

"What did you do", she whispered, hanging on to his every word.

He continued to stare ahead, a teardrop rolling down his cheek. "It was an act of mercy. I…I…" he choked, "I gave her an overdose of her painkillers. What was left in the bottle. She left us a few hours later."

His face crumpled, the tears welled up, and he broke down, sobbing uncontrollably.

## Daphne's daffodils

"Oh no" she shrieked. "What has become of you, my darlings?"

Daphne stared in horror at the shredded daffodils which had been scattered over her allotment beds and the adjacent paths separating her patch from others. Joan Riddlesdown was kneeling on her plot, weeding by the looks of things. "Joan," she screamed, "Have you seen what has been done to my daffodils? Come and take a look."

Joan rose to her feet and threaded her way along the footpath towards her, but stopped before she reached where Daphne was standing. "Oh my goodness," Joan yelped, with left hand to her mouth, and staring down at something. Unlike her, Joan had never been heard to curse, or utter anything remotely resembling a profanity. "Daphne, you need to see this. Bill's cabbages, or what's left of them."

Daphne wandered over to where Joan was standing beside Bill's allotment. Unusually for this time of the day, Bill was not around. The piercing cries of the two of them had alerted other members. Nigel came over, as did Stacey and a couple of others. They were standing round exchanging ever mounting expressions of incredulity when Bill Southwick appeared. Unlike Joan, Daphne was not one to hold back her feelings. She was quite certain who had perpetrated the assault on her daffodils and Bill's cabbages. Her wrath exploded and she launched into a tirade of abuse about Hugo Wivelsfield.

***************

The wanton destruction of her daffodils had released her pent-up fury, tapping into a wellspring of bitterness going back many years since the divorce from her husband. Wrath and fury pretty much summarised Daphne Littlehampton. Her life, her ex-husband, her quarrels with anyone and everyone, more latterly concentrated around the allotment plots.

She had left school at fifteen. Pretty much everyone in her class and social circle had done so, as one did in those days. The only career advice she had received from her form teacher, Miss Summersby, was to either train as a secretary or find a good husband. Daphne had trialled both, although the second had not been entirely successful. She had found the husband, but 'good' should not have been attached to 'husband', although she was not to find this out until a considerable period of their marriage had elapsed

Growing up in the Home Counties, as the youngest child and with three elder brothers, Daphne had enjoyed a comfortable life in a well to do family. Her father was something or other in property and they lived in a rambling detached house with sizeable grounds. In her late teenage years, Daphne's social life had revolved around the county set and the Young Conservatives, and though not attractive in the conventional sense, she had no shortage of suitors. Tall for a young woman of her age and with a haughty – and behind her back some said horsey – demeanour, she took part in the normal activities of the county, or at least those activities that had been normal for her social set in those times.

After completing her training, she had progressed through a series of secretarial roles, ending up as personal secretary to the managing director of a large property company in the City of London. It was there that she met and married the man who became her husband. She could hardly fail to have met David Littlehampton, as she saw him most days in her role. She knew he had been previously married, but he had told her it was when they were both early twenties and far too young.

After marriage, David had been a faithful and attentive husband as far as she was aware, but had insisted that her rightful role was to look after the home and organise their social affairs where these did not revolve around the office. Daphne had offered little resistance, bored as she was with her working life, now that she had met her career ambition in the shape of her good husband. Although they had both wanted children, it was not to be.

Nearly twenty years of largely uneventful married life had come and gone when completely out of the blue one evening just before Christmas, David had announced peremptorily that he was leaving her for a younger model, as he put it. In fact it soon turned out that the new paramour was a TV gameshow hostess rather than a model, but younger she most certainly was. Daphne had at the start been determined to fight the divorce decreed by her husband's decision, but had eventually agreed, following advice by her lawyer, to accept the settlement offer. Only years later did she find out that the lawyer and her by then ex-husband had been officers of the same Masonic lodge. It rankled then how she had been short-changed, and still did some twenty years later.

She returned to live nearer where she had been brought up. A friend of her father's had found her a secretarial position, which at least secured a regular income, although not the lifestyle she had previously enjoyed. Needing something to occupy herself after takeover of the business, followed by redundancy, a girl friend had suggested she take on an allotment. Daphne had managed to obtain a small plot through her friend's connections.

Although to start with she had not the faintest idea of what was entailed in working an allotment plot, she had over time learned to grow both vegetables and flowers with the assistance and advice of some of the more experienced members, particularly Bill and Joan. Daffodils were her pride and joy, the roses never doing very much despite much advice from others. The daffodils seemed to smile at her on every visit when they were in bloom.

Having been a hearty carnivore since childhood, for reasons she could never quite fathom Daphne had become a vegetarian since divorce and the procurement of the allotment. Furthermore, since the change in her dietary habits she had also changed the diet of her dog to eat only vegetarian produce, more usually carrots and tomatoes from the allotment when they were in season.

Winnie, named after her father's hero Winston Churchill, was frequently sick, but Daphne never connected this practice to its nutritional regime. Unbeknown to her, some of Daphne's fellow allotment holders made great fun of the dog, but never in her presence. Daphne's renowned quick temper and unrivalled capacity for verbal abuse forestalled anyone tempted to indiscretion.

"That Hugo has something going with Stacey," she opined forcefully one day to Joan. They had popped over to the 'Original Oak' for a drink, prior to going their separate ways to their respective homes.

"Really?" said Joan, placing her schooner of sherry back on the table. "Whatever makes you think that?"

"It's their body language, and the way they look at each other."

"Do you really think so?" Joan asked in a tone suggesting she didn't really believe or want to believe what she was hearing.

"Course he has. They have. They're as bad as each other."

"Stacey, she's such a nice woman. Always stops for a natter. We don't see so much of Clive these days, do we, but they seemed such a devoted couple back in the day when they used to be together on their plot."

Joan's wide-eyed innocence tickled her.

"Don't be so naïve, Joan. Devoted they may be, but not to each other," she spluttered, spraying the majority of a mouthful of Dubonnet almost into Joan's face. "Mark my words, there's some hanky-panky between those two. I should know."

"What do you mean?"

"Hanky panky. You know, illiterate goings on." Daphne was getting so carried away that she mangled her words.

"Yes, I know what hanky-panky is, thank you," Joan replied, "I meant, how should you know?"

"Because I went through it with my ex-husband, with…with.." Even after all the passage of time, Daphne could not bring herself to mention his name. "..that bounder."

"Oh, I see." Joan paused, clearly unsure about pressing her for more information.

"He left me for a TV hostess. A slut. All fur and no knickers. He never did have any taste or breeding…Apart from marrying me, of course," Daphne hurriedly corrected herself. "And he left me with so little money. He swindled me out of my rightful share. After all, I organised the home and all our social arrangements all those years. He left me all but a pauper, diddled me out of what was rightfully mine, with that conniving solicitor pal. Still, I survive," she said defiantly, the stream of bile temporarily ceasing.

She felt Joan's hand on her arm. "You poor dear. It's not right." Joan said, trying to console her.

"Oh my goodness. Just look at the time. Is it that late? Must fly, need to go home and feed the cats."

She rose, swallowed the remaining contents of the glass, and tugged at the dog who had been lying patiently under the table. "Come on Winnie, let's go and feed your housemates." And with that, she swept out of the pub.

Daphne walked back home, Winnie ambling alongside. The house with its three bedrooms was overlarge for her needs. Although she lived alone in the sense of being the only human occupant, the presence of one dog and three cats went some way to making up for the absence of other humans. In truth their presence may have gone some of the way, but she was very conscious of the void in her life which had existed for twenty years or so. Had anyone visited the house, not that she had permitted anyone to cross the threshold for many years, they would have been affronted by the state it was in, and the smell deriving from a combination of the habits of semi house-trained feral cats and the lack of regular and thorough housekeeping.

Daphne wandered into the gloomy hall and took off her coat, which had seen better days; much better days. One of the cats rubbed against her leg and meowed plaintively. "Now, now. Din dins is on its way," she cooed as she picked up the rather unkempt furry bundle. "Have you been lonely without me?"

After opening the tins of cat food – for whatever reason, unlike with Winnie, she did not confine them to a vegetarian diet – she went upstairs to the bathroom to wash the allotment soil off her hands. Her reflection in the bathroom mirror stared back at her. Although never having been good looking in the conventional sense, there still remained the remnants of the allure that had once made her attractive to the opposite sex. Now the classy hauteur of her younger self had long since faded and her wrinkled visage displayed the impact of her lonely existence, compounded by the daily intake of too much alcoholic drink.

Most days were like today. A session working on the allotment, a drink or three in the comfort of her shed or in the pub, and return to the house devoid of any human company, followed by a glass of port or two. It was a lonely life, brightened only by her cats and dog, and the opportunities for gossip at the expense of her fellow allotment holders.

Since the events of the AGM and the destruction of her daffodils, Daphne had spent more time inside the shed on her plot. Shed was a somewhat grandiose description of the wooden construction, which someone unbeknown to her had termed Daphne's dirty den. It squatted in the centre of her plot, brooding over the surrounding area like the remote moorland building from a Bronte novel. Bill and Nigel had helped her build the shed, or more truthfully carried out all the work, pillaging the wooden planks which formed the walls and the corrugated iron sheets which comprised the roof from nearby skips. Through gaps and knot-holes sited in each of the four walls, she could cast a mistrustful eye in every compass direction over the allotments, and its various comings and goings.

One day, it could have been any day such was the mundanity of her routine, she sat in her shed, a beaker in her hand, peering out through one of her spyholes. She watched intently as Hugo and Stacey cultivated their respective allotments, seemingly concentrating on the task at hand. However the occasional discrete glance at each other suggested a different scenario. Her teeth grated. As she continued to sit and watch, Joan wandered into view, carrying a watering can towards the tap. Daphne stood up, and poked her head out of the door of the shed. "Joan, come over here for a minute," she hollered.

Joan looked up.

"Let me just get rid of this," she called back, and walked over to her plot with her watering can, obviously full judging by the way Joan lurched to one side. Joan emptied the can and came over to the shed.

"What is it?" Joan asked.

"Come inside for a minute and watch what happens." Joan entered the shed and looked out. After a short time, Hugo and Stacey sloped off to all appearances independently, separated by barely a minute or so.

"What did I tell you? There you are. I told you there was something going on between that pair," Daphne exhaled, a distinct note of triumph in her voice.

"Well it could just be coincidence," Joan replied, plainly wanting to give them the benefit of her doubt.

"Not a bit of it. They're off for a bit of rumpy-pumpy."

"Even if they are, so what? It's their affair, and none of our business," Joan said, sounding more convincing than Daphne suspected was the reality.

"Affair it most certainly is. It's disgusting. And Stacey Portslade, a married woman at that Think of her poor husband. He comes here so rarely these days, probably because he knows what is going on. I've a good mind to give them what for."

"But why? Why are you so fixated with them? That business at the AGM? What is it to you? Why do you work yourself up so much?"

"It's…Well…Oh you're right as usual, Joan. I say, let's have a snifter." And with that, Daphne poured each of them a generous measure from the grimy bottle on the shelf of the shed. They engaged in small talk for a while. Daphne was aware of Joan quite deliberately steering the conversation away from the topic of Hugo and Stacey. A few more generous beakerfuls of sherry ensued. By this time, Daphne felt the effect of the alcohol taking its toll, although Joan gave every appearance of being none the worse for wear.

"It's strange, isn't it," Joan said after a brief period of silence that they had both fallen in to.

"What is?"

"The two of us sitting here, and drinking in the middle of the afternoon. Strange." Joan looked down at the beaker in her hand. "How did we end up like this?"

"It wouldn't have been my preferred choice, I can tell you!" Daphne said morosely, in turn staring down at her drink. "Events, dear girl. Events quite beyond my control."

"Well I can understand. You went through a lot," said Joan. The story of Daphne's marital break-up being a well-worn and all too frequent topic of much of their conversation.

"I did," said Daphne, her gaze fixed on her glass.

"Yes you did. Your ex-husband has a lot to answer for. Is that why you are obsessed with

Hugo? Does he remind you of your ex-husband?"

There was another silence. Daphne looked up, startled. "You don't know the half of it." She spat out the words, and then crumpled, an imploding shell of her normal loud and bombastic persona.

"What do you mean?" Joan said softly.

Daphne stopped and pondered whether to carry on with what was on her mind. "Joan, did you ever want children?"

There was now in turn a lengthy pregnant pause on Joan's part. "Why, did you?" Joan eventually responded, parrying the question.

Even after all the sherry, Joan's avoidance of the question penetrated her consciousness. Daphne decided not to follow this up, but deal with the question batted back to her. "Of course I wanted children. I always wanted children."

"But… why didn't you have them? I know the breakup of your marriage must have been difficult, but you were still fairly young, young enough to meet someone else and have children." Joan responded, the nervousness in her manner all too evident.

"Well it wasn't just that. Well it was but there was a lot more besides."

Joan was on the verge of saying something, but stopped and waited for Daphne to carry on.

"We both wanted children…and we tried." Daphne paused. "Eventually we went to see the specialist." Daphne paused again. "Apparently I had some gynaecological condition that prevented me from conceiving."

"Oh, you poor thing. At least you still had your husband…." Joan said, oblivious at first to what she had said. "Well, what I meant was..." It was too late to correct what had been said. "I'm sorry. Wrong thing to say."

"I didn't have my husband. He abandoned me for a brazen hussy," Daphne exploded.

"I know," Joan said quietly, desperately aware of the virtual hole she had dug for herself. "You must have..."

Daphne looked up, all of a sudden, and stared straight at Joan, tears welling up in her eyes. "It's more. Much more." She paused, uncertain as to whether she could or wanted to carry on. Even in her semi-drunken state, she was fully aware of what she was saying. After all this time, it was time to tell someone.

"You see, after we had seen the specialist, we were devastated. At least, I was. Eventually I went to see someone, to see if there was some form of medical alternative, but there wasn't. The only option was adoption. So we went to an adoption agency. They interviewed us, and inspected our home. We were all set; they had found a little boy…" She paused again, shaking so much that the chair vibrated against the inside of the shed. There was a question on the tip of Joan's tongue, but before she could get the words out, Daphne carried on "…the next week, he told me he was leaving me. So it all fell apart."

Emotions unleashed, the floodgate of tears opened and she fell off the chair on to the ground, convulsed in anguish. Joan helped her to her feet, embraced her, and then burst into tears herself. They clutched one another, and clung together, Daphne in desolation, Joan in devastation. Neither knew what more to say, so they both sat in silence.

Eventually, and with some difficulty, Daphne broke the leaden silence. "Thanks for listening, Joan," she said, unusually softly for her," it's been a long time. I have never talked about this to anyone before. Perhaps you should go. I just want to be alone with my thoughts."

Joan stood up, hugged Daphne, and departed, wending her way along the allotment paths and back to her home, dazed and uncertain how to process what she had heard.

It was already dusk and Daphne lit a candle to provide some light in the shed. She sat down again and felt for the bottle. Her hand grasped the neck of a plastic container on the floor, unscrewed the top, and poured another measure of the brown liquid.

That was the last thing she remembered, until she woke up several hours later with a start. And a throbbing headache. Night had fallen and she eventually worked out through the fog of her dazed state that she was still in the shed at her allotment, if rather the worse for wear.

Lurching to her feet, she staggered to the doorway and looked out. The sky was clear and the moon shone brightly. Even in her inebriated state, she observed that it was larger than normal and appeared ruddy brown in colour. She thought she saw a figure in the distance moving closer towards her on an adjacent path, but dismissed it as a figment of her alcohol fuelled imagination.

She moved back inside the shed and turned to sit down. The moonlight spilling through the doorway all of a sudden faded. Startled, she glanced up. There was a silhouette of a figure standing in the doorway.

## Joan's rhubarb

Joan ascribed the success of her prize-winning rhubarb to the large chimney pot lovingly retrieved from a skip that she had driven past one day in Buxton, on a visit to see her elder sister. Perhaps the soot gathered from her sister's coal fire – rare in these times - also provided an essential contribution.

She convinced herself she had managed to retain the figure of her youth, perhaps not unrelated to her allotment endeavours. No doubt the exercise in carrying gallons of water in her watering can from the butt to her plot, and the lifting and shifting of the chimney pot might have played a part she fantasised, notwithstanding her partiality to a tipple of Fino sherry.

It was readily agreed that she was one of those people all allotments need, the glue that helped the rest of the allotment association to bond. No-one could recall her ever having a bad word to say about any of her fellow members, and she was always available to proffer advice. Joan Riddlesdown was a good egg. Together with Bill Southwick, she effectively ran the association; him as chairman, her as secretary.

"Morning Nigel," she called to Nigel Hassocks one Saturday morning as she walked through the allotment grounds to her own plot. Joan and Nigel were both in full-time jobs and consequently tended to work on the allotments mostly at weekends, except for the late spring and summer when extended daylight hours meant they could work into the evenings.

"Morning Joan," he called back, head slightly lifting from his bent position as he dug away on his plot. "I'm on late shift this week, so getting some work in before I I have to go and sort out the troublemakers. And after my police colleagues, I have to deal with the criminals!" A braying sound which she assumed to be an attempt to laugh at his own words followed.

"Now, now Nigel. Pots and kettles." Nigel is on good form, she thought, as she continued on to her plot. It was a pleasant morning, cool but with a bright full sun already high in the azure blue sky, despite the relative early hour.

"Oh to be in an English allotment, now that April is here," she thought to herself, paraphrasing Browning, although April had come and gone and there was no chaffinch singing nor any orchard bough. Joan nevertheless felt some degree of careless rapture. Another week of school term over, and the weekend to recover and recharge batteries, ready for the challenges of the next week.

Joan had been born and brought up in a Derbyshire mining area, although by the time she went to university many of the mines had closed or were on borrowed time. Her father worked for the local council and her mother was a teacher, as had been her mother's mother, so it was natural for Joan to follow her family's calling. She taught English at a local comprehensive, formerly the grammar school until the changes in education policy after the 1960's.

She had moved south to take up a head of department post. Fifteen years ago, she found teaching to be stimulating and motivating. Now it had become fraught and stressful, the result of constant government changes, pressure to achieve measurable but unattainable outcomes, volumes of paperwork and reports, and the dreaded Ofsted inspections. So much so, that she had begun to count down the days to retirement, now within her sights.

Marriage had eluded her, not that she had intentionally either sought or steered clear of it. There had been a couple of longer-term relationships and the odd shorter one, but for whatever reason things had not worked out in the way she might have desired. There had been that fellow teacher in one of her first schools, but he had moved on to another job. And that was that. Alone again, naturally.

She had yearned to bring up children of her own, but circumstances had conspired against her. On further thought, as she often used to think, not so much a conspiracy, merely events. Not that she talked about those days, these days. There had been the odd moment when she had wanted to open up, but something deep within her had always held her in check.

The allotment provided a haven of retreat from the weekday teaching pressures, an island of solace in a sea of ferment. She enjoyed the company of her fellow members, some more than others, and relied on the activities of allotment routine for much of her social life.

Although she was a member of an amateur dramatic society, and took in the occasional theatre and opera visit with a neighbour, outside of school the allotment was where she focussed her efforts.

Together with Bill Southwick, she ran the allotment committee, and had been drawn closer to Bill through their joint venture as committee officers. She knew that Bill had found it difficult to cope with the death of his wife, from which she thought he had never recovered. Although neither of them had said anything to the other, something had developed between them over the course of the past couple of years or so. From time to time, as she sat down to rest from her allotment exertions, she would mull over her feelings about Bill.

What was it? Affection? Certainly. Attraction? Not in a physical sense maybe, but there again she felt something. Attachment? Having not felt attached to anyone else for large periods of her life, she could not be sure what it meant. But there was a something there. She experienced a warmth and comfort in close proximity, whether on the allotment or in the committee meetings, tortuous though they usually were.

Bill's most valued contribution was to dig over her patch when required. Joan struggled to apply sufficient downward force on the spade to enable the soil to be turned over, probably she guessed the first signs of the onset of arthritis in her knees. One day, Bill had offered his services as she laboured in vain, and had done more in an hour than she would have done in days. She surreptitiously eyed his muscular biceps peeking out from his rolled-up shirt sleeves, as they stretched and bulged, admiring the restrained dignity and understated nobility of his physical labour

"There we go," he said, leaning back, foot on spade, to gaze with a quiet satisfaction on the results of his endeavours. "That looks better. Those brambles are a devil to remove. Careful you don't scratch yourself, mind."

"Many thanks, Bill. You're a real treasure. I don't know what I would do without you," she responded, carefully avoiding eye contact.

"You've a champion crop of rhubarb, I'll say. That chimney pot obviously helps to force the crop and keep it nice and straight. None of this foreign bent stuff."

"Bill, I don't know about that. I doubt that Europe has much to do with it, if that's what you mean. Soot, that's my secret. Nothing but old-fashioned soot. My sister up north has a coal fire, and brings me a supply of soot when she comes to visit. I don't know how she gets away with a coal fire these days, but she does."

"You're right there," he confirmed. "Not really a secret, though, otherwise the rhubarb triangle would never have developed. They used night soil and muck from t'woollen mills, mind."

"Night soil, what's that, Bill?"

"Surely tha knows?"

"No, I have no idea."

"You surprise me. It's human excrement. Shit by any other name."

"Oh, I see. And what's this about the rhubarb triangle, Bill? Is this another of your fanciful northern fables?"

"Not a bit of it. Tha' knows nowt. Happen you come from Derby, but that's Midlands like."

"Derbyshire, actually. And most people in the south think Derbyshire is in the north," she said, warming to the friendly banter.

"Any road. Did you know, Joan, that ninety percent of the world's rhubarb used to be grown in a small area of Yorkshire. Aye, the Rhubarb Triangle, they call it. Between Leeds, Bradford and Wakefield."

"Bill, you're having me on."

"I'm not. Wakefield still has a rhubarb festival when last I heard, and there's also a rhubarb statue."

"A rhubarb statue? A statue made of rhubarb? April Fool's Day may have come and gone, but you are having me on."

"No, one of those things carved out of stone or summat in the shape of rhubarb."

"Oh, you mean a sculpture."

"Yes, that's it. Done by a famous local man."

"Not Henry Moore?" she uttered in astonishment.

"Henry Moore? Didn't he used to do that programme on the television about the sky at night?"

"Bill, I think that was Patrick Moore."

"Happen. Anyroad, I read somewhere that rhubarb growing in Yorkshire is even protected by Europe, or perhaps was."

"Now I know you're having me on."

"Look it up. See for thissen. It's same as Stilton cheese and Parma ham. Even Champagne."

"Champagne and rhubarb! That's a bizarre combination," she said, laughing in delight at his earnest manner and dogged conviction. "Tell you what, I'll give you some of my rhubarb when it's ready. You can have it with your champagne."

Now it was his turn to laugh. "Champagne! All those bubbles and fizz." He paused for a moment. "Mind you, there was a time when Brenda was partial to a bottle of Babycham." He stopped, and there was an awkward silence.

"There, there," she said, touching him on the arm.

"Aye," he said, seemingly stifling a tear. "We'd best get back to work. See'ya later." And with that, he strolled off, back to his plot.

She bent down and pulled out a couple of weed roots that Bill had missed, her crucifix necklace hovering just above the soil. Slowly and with some effort she straightened and stood up, looking around at Bill's reassuring form retreating in to the distance.

Most weekends, Joan's habitual practice was to arrive reasonably early at the allotment, and labour through to lunch time, with the occasional break for coffee prepared at home and kept warm in the Thermos flask which she took with her. Lunch took one of several options, perhaps a visit to the café or an occasional pub lunch if she was in the mood and could find an accomplice. Stacey she liked, warm and kind. Nigel she trusted, an upstanding pillar of the community being a police officer after all. Even Daphne for heaven's sake, if you could ignore the slings and arrows of her all too felt outraged misfortune, could occasionally be willingly tempted.

In the absence of a willing companion, she used her battered but functioning Primus stove to cook up bacon. The whiff of paraffin wafting through her small shed somehow seemed to her to be the perfect aperitif to the sizzling aroma of lightly fried streaky bacon rashers which she then carefully placed in thick slices of fluffy white bread to create her perfect lunchtime sandwich. The stove was a relic of her Girl Guide days and weekend hikes in the Peak District. Not that she did much hiking these days, what with her knees. The allotment more than satisfied her need for exercise.

How she loved to bury her teeth in the hefty doorstep of a bacon sandwich. Or commonly two, with generous helpings of brown sauce, a legacy of her northern – or Midlands - origins. She gorged on the sandwiches, as she gorged on most food nowadays. It was hard to recall precisely when it had started, but she had from nowhere acquired an insatiable urge to stuff herself with food. More accurately, a ravenous desire to graze, gnash and nibble between mealtimes.

If her gluttony had been confined to regular meals, as it once had been, there would have been less of a problem. Now there was. She used to fit into a size eight, more likely a size ten if the mist of time past was dispelled, but now it had become size fourteen. Whereas once there was a slim, sylph like younger model, it had been overgrown by a well-rounded middle-aged design. Well rounded? In her dreams. More plump in truth.

****************

Late one afternoon, as the earlier sun had vanished behind a thickish layer of cloud producing a gloom that belied the remaining hours of daylight, she spotted Nigel Hassocks on his plot, staring at Hugo departing from the allotment ground. "Fancy an afternoon brew, Nigel," she called out. He turned as if startled out of some deep and meaningful reverie.

"Why not. Don't mind if I do," he answered, and proceeded at a steady pace over to her plot. "Do we have cucumber sandwiches as well?" he chortled.

Joan smiled. "Not today. I've eaten them all up."

"Shame. I could just throttle a cucumber sandwich for afternoon tea. Plug a gap. I've half a mind to pinch one of Stacey's remaining crop, before they rot. I doubt she'd miss just the one."

"And you a police officer, at that. Well, you'll just have to resist that temptation and wait for your evening meal," she said, more aggressively than intended."

"Detective, police detective, plain clothes branch," corrected Nigel.

"When I called over just now, you looked miles away?"

"Was I? Probably thinking about a current case, or just daydreaming. Nothing more than that."

"Really? Pound to a penny you had other things on your mind, given the way you were gaping at Hugo?"

"Could be," he muttered, tentatively.

"What's up. What is it? Envy, jealousy, contempt?"

"Some people have all the luck, don't you think?" he said, determinedly, and with some passion.

"Well…maybe." Now it was she who was muttering.

"What do you mean?" he said, enquiringly. "Life's been good to you, hasn't it?"

It was the suddenness of the question, coming out of nowhere, that jolted her out of thoughts of the present. She would never know why those memories of the past were dislodged from the depths of her being, where they had been hidden for so long.

"No it bloody well hasn't," she blurted out, burying her face in her hands.

"What do you mean?" he repeated, now more kindly, bewildered by the change in her demeanour. "Why don't you sit down. I'll make tea."

Joan realised too late that there was no escape, no turning back, as she sat down on one of the rickety chairs that had seen better days, much like her, she opined. All of a sudden, she was on the edge of something. She watched him pump up the Primus, boil the water, and pour it over the Tetley teabags he had placed in the two rather grubby mugs.

"There we go," he said, handing one of the mugs of tea to her. "All life's problems are magicked away with a cup of tea."

"If only that were so. If only…" She paused, even more hesitant than a few moments ago.

"Well, you see," she paused again. It was as if she was on the edge of a precipice: she could go back, but felt she had already exposed something of herself; the only alternative was to head onward, over the edge. She decided to go forwards.

"You're happily married, Nigel, are you not?"

If she had not been totally overwhelmed by her own thoughts, she would surely have noticed the momentary reluctance to respond immediately.

"Yes, of course," he replied after a pause.

"And you and your wife have children, haven't you?"

"You know we have," he answered.

"Of course I do." She paused, and then continued hesitantly." You see, I always wanted a child."

"It's fine. You don't have to go on," he said, somewhat embarrassed and not sure where this was leading. "After all, we are friends but I'm not that good with these things," he offered lamely, as a hopefully perceived genuine expression.

Inside himself, naturally he wanted her to go on to see where this was going. It was like listening to a suspect, on the verge of a critical admission. He could always tell when someone was about to crack. After years of experience, it came with the territory.

"No, that's why I can go on. You are a police officer, and I trust you, trust you that it will go no further. Especially with Daphne. I have wanted to tell someone for an eternity. "

She paused again, then dived into her emotional abyss. "There was this man, a long time ago. We had a relationship, and I …."

Nigel said nothing. That also came with experience. Don't interrupt a silence.

She resumed, "I..I got pregnant. It was..it was careless of me. I hadn't taken the pill, for some reason. Maybe that was not accidental. Maybe intentional. " The words were spewing out at an increasing rate.

"What happened? Was there a problem with the birth?" he had to fill the gap in her delivery, desperate for her to reach the denouement of her story.

"No…well yes. This man, he was married. I had hoped he might leave his wife for me, but he wouldn't. Religious upbringing he said, which I understood."

"Oh," said Nigel. "So did you, you know, like, erm, end the pregnancy?" he said, avoiding the word that was on the tip of his tongue.

"No. I'm Catholic, and couldn't bring myself at that stage to have a termination. I went ahead and gave birth. A boy. He was so beautiful, but I couldn't face bringing up a child on my own in those days, without any support. My parents were still alive, but I did not dare to tell them. They would have been so shocked. A child with no attending father, and me unmarried. So I tried to arrange an adoption."

"I see."

"There was this couple who were keen to adopt him. I never knew their names or met them. He was in property apparently. But something happened to them. I never found out what it was. They couldn't go ahead with the adoption, or so the agency told me. So sad." She slumped on the chair in silence, staring straight ahead, her eyes fixed on some horizon.

Nigel said nothing.

Once more, she carried on. "I was devastated, but couldn't face another round of it, with further possible disappointment."

Again, Nigel said nothing.

"It was probably my hormones. They were all over the place. I felt I couldn't carry on."

Nigel sat stock still, absolutely stunned, fearing where the story would end. "So what happened?" he eventually said. He had to say something. He could feel his heart racing, the tension unbearable, although he had a hint of a suspicion of where this was going.

"I eventually left him on the doorstep of a children's home," she said quietly, in a matter-of-fact voice. "I never saw him again. I couldn't face myself with what I had done, or anyone else for that matter. Now and again, I wonder what it would be like to find him after all this time, but I wouldn't know where to begin."

He was about to respond that he was a detective and had certain skills likely to be of value, but saw her distraught face and thought better of it. Some things are best left unsaid.

"So there it is. Now you know."

"Now I know," he nodded. "You poor thing," and reached out to hold her hand.

## Nigel's coriander

As a relative newcomer to the allotment world with all its rituals and traditions, Nigel knew that the green-leaved plants barely visible through the murky greenhouse windows might arouse questions, but his self-assurance overcame any reservation that lurked inside him. For some reason, he had a misplaced sense of his own infallibility; he was free of doubt, beyond suspicion, untouchable. Naturally, he was beyond suspicion – he was a member of His Majesty's constabulary.

Detective Sergeant Nigel Hassocks reporting for duties. Age: early fifties. Appearance: six-foot plus, gangly build, straggly hair, florid face. A pair of metal-framed spectacles perched on the end of his bulbous nose, perennially threatening to break free and fall off. Marital status: married with three children, youngest still living at home. Previous career: soldier in armed services, served in Northern Ireland and first Gulf War. Pastimes: watching sport on television, working on his recently acquired allotment plot. Bad habits: none he would care to admit, at least in public and in front of witnesses.

That was the key point, he often thought aloud to himself. None that he would care to admit. Modern society with its openness and lack of privacy was a companion living cheek by jowl, but his association was very much at arms' length. His children, from what he could gather by way of snatched titbits from earwigged conversations, seemed to delight in baring their souls and he suspected more physical attributes to the world at large through social media.

Not that he understood anything about the apparent attractions of Facebook, Twitter, Instamatic and various other channels he heard bandied about. Turning yourself inside out to the wider world, that was not his way. As a police officer that would also not be wise. He was required to give evidence in court, and had a robust occupational disrespect for the legal profession. The less anyone could find out about him, the better it would be.

He temporarily paused the turning of his compost heap, lifted his left foot off the spade, and reached into his right-hand trouser pocket, pulling out the packet of Benson and Hedges nestling there. He extracted a cigarette, lit it and stood back to draw in a lungful of the worst that tobacco and its tars could pitch at him. Nigel looked about him to see who was around. Bill was present, as normal, as was Daphne. At the far end, he could see another couple, but couldn't recall their names. Just as he bent down to carry on, he spied Stacey walking up the path towards him.

"Hello Nigel," she said, stopping as she reached him. "How is the coriander doing?"

"It's coming on. Still needs more time and attention." He suspected he knew why everyone seemed to be curious about his plants.

"I just can't understand what you are doing with it. I've never heard of anyone protecting coriander in a heated greenhouse in summer. Mind you, the leaves from what I can see of them are much larger than the usual sort of coriander. And the aroma, quite distinctive."

"Yes, that's right. It's a rather special variety, not the usual bog-standard coriander. It's Vietnamese coriander, it needs warmth and close protection," he said, hoping that his voice of authority would put an end to the matter. Was there a speculative aspect to Stacey's gently probing interrogation, he wondered? He thought he had succeeded in keeping his tone steady and free of any unease about the line of her questioning, such that he could safely move the conversational topic on to safer ground.

"How's things with you? I haven't seen much of you lately. Tell the truth, I haven't been here much myself recently. I've been on day shifts and dealing with a major organised crime investigation. Very tricky and complex, so not managed to get down here very often."

"I'm fine," she murmured, in a flat voice devoid of any expressiveness.

Was there a hint of discomfort in her answer, he wondered to himself.

"How's Clive? Not seen him at all for many weeks?"

"No, he's been busy at work as ever. He always seems to be, these days. You know what lawyers are like with their bundles and briefs. I have hardly seen him myself. Now, must get to work. Those weeds will strangle my cucumbers and courgettes unless I deal with them." And with that, she strode on down the path to her own plot.

Definite discomfort, now he thought. His eyes followed her. He took another draw of his cigarette, and watched Stacey's shapely form recede into the distance, with what seemed to be an excessively exaggerated swaying of her hips. Was this intended to taunt or excite him? Whether or not, it was certainly successful. He continued to stare at her, transfixed. Her lustrous blonde hair, tossed by hip motion, shimmered in the late afternoon sun. God, she was gorgeous. How he envied Clive. Some men have all the luck,

"Hope for your sake the wind doesn't change. Your eyes are popping out so far I could hang my hat on them"

He didn't need to turn round to recognise the provenance of the squawk, followed by a burst of laughter, emanating from the adjacent plot. Startled, he felt his face flushing with the embarrassment that his thoughts were so palpably naked to others. How had he not spotted Daphne Littlehampton's presence? It invariable announced itself, as it had on this occasion.

"Actually I was looking at the state of the path by that Hugo's allotment," he expounded lamely. He knew it was unconvincing. It even sounded lame to him.

"No you weren't! You were fantasising about Stacey over there. Stands out a mile, as one might say."

Without a second thought, he glanced down instinctively at his lower body and then corrected himself, suddenly conscious that his action could be uncharitably interpreted as an affirmation of Daphne's lewd remark.

"No I wasn't," he stammered, feeling his cheeks burning as if acid had been thrown at them. "I was looking at the path, and how the grass has erupted. All the recent rain means it needs attention. That Hugo needs to get down more often."

"I'm sure he has been getting down often enough with Mrs Portslade," came the rejoinder with the emphasis on the Mrs, followed by a cackling guffaw. "They're at it together. That's why his path is overgrown and his allotment in need of more care and attention." And with that, Daphne wandered off.

Like some of the other members, Nigel had observed the body language and evident signs of evolving intimacy between Stacey and Hugo. His police training and instincts told him that they left the allotment apparently with separate intent, but within a short interval of time there would be joint enterprise. How he envied Hugo.

Although his marriage to Margaret was solid enough, that one-off with the young PC apart, Nigel could not dispel the envy he felt. Stacey was a stunner. Any man would be forgiven for harbouring covetous desires for her. But that Hugo? He was nothing, nothing but a shallow chancer. He had come across many of his like in the course of his duties. He looked up for Stacey, but she had disappeared from view, and rather wistfully returned to his labours.

Nigel habitually wore shorts on the allotment, even in the depths of mid-winter. Held up by bright carmine-coloured braces, the shorts rode high on his spindly frame, hanging over his sticklike legs, giving him from a certain angle the profile of a severely malnourished stick insect. Today like most spring and summer days, he had stripped to the waist, his shirt hung over one of the forks.

Unbeknown to him, this deportment had been subject to scathing asides from other members, or at least one in particular. 'An affront to scarecrows', was one of Daphne's more scathing comments. On colder days he wore a long tweed-brown coat, which flowed out behind him as he strode purposely in his battered gardening shoes, along the main path separating the plots. Hugo Wivelsfield had waggishly and memorably described his appearance – away from Nigel's hearing - as the Doctor Who of Planet Helleborus. Jokes tended to travel far on allotments, and this one had journeyed further than most.

Not that sympathy should be over-extended in his direction. He himself was not above proffering the occasionally witty but more often snide and gratuitous remarks behind the backs of fellow members. Nigel referred to Daphne's small dog as Winnie the Poo, a name which caused much mirth and had been readily adopted by Bill and other members. The nickname had come to mind one day when a particularly odorous piece of excrement, doubtlessly resulting from its weird vegetarian diet he surmised, had been deposited by the dog on one of the pathways. Naturally no-one had the courage to use the sobriquet in Daphne's formidable presence or within earshot.

He avoided Daphne where and when possible, aware that she was a fearful gossip and busybody, liable to insert her oar into every rowlock of everyday allotment activity.On an allotment where members had to share use of facilities such as water, it was however difficult to keep his distance from her. With most of the other members, he felt more comfortable and valued the sharing of tips and advice. He knew a bit about Bill Southwick and Joan Riddlesdown, although he would in time to come be astounded by Joan's secret and the fact that she had volunteered this to him.

Hugo was one of a kind; smooth, smarmy, obviously privately schooled, not his type but no other evidence to be held against him, other than an intense jealousy of Hugo's easy manner and presumed success with ladies in general and Stacey in particular. Deep down, he envied Hugo as the kind of man he had once aspired to be. Effortlessly superior, a supreme confidence bordering on arrogance and to all appearances extremely successful.

\*\*\*\*\*\*\*\*\*\*\*\*\*\*\*\*

Allotment activity was a round of seasonal routines and activities. Cultivating the plot; digging, planting, weeding, hoeing, thinning out, fertilising, watering, cropping, and tending to the compost heap. Ah, the compost heap. Surprisingly, this was one of the allotment tasks that he thought most about. Bill had warned him that one of the worrying things that happened on the allotments was the nicking of manure, compost and fertiliser. Maybe it was his professional antennae being ultra-sensitive, but Nigel sensed that Bill had mentioned the thefts to him quite deliberately, fully conscious of his role in nicking thiefs. Really, he worked long shifts as it was and had no desire to spread his activity into catching compost criminals.

The compost heap was nevertheless something of a fixation with him, and tt was one of the few things that kept him awake at night. And for very good reason. He had read in some weekend supplement or internet website somewhere, he couldn't recall which, that peeing on the muck helped to activate the composting process. At his stage of life, and with his enlarged prostate, that offered the prospect of killing two birds with one pebble. Or two B's with one P, he thought, amused at his own wit.

While he had no intention of a daily pee on his compost heap, Nigel did want to test out the theory with a trial run, so to speak. He wondered to himself how he could manage this without being accosted for indecency. As a police officer, and a sergeant at that, he could not afford the risk and potential public opprobrium. Plainly such an act could not be accomplished in daylight without the chance that someone would see what he was doing. So it was that one evening, he announced to his wife after the ten o'clock news had finished that he had to pop out.

"Where are you going at this time of night?" was the fairly predictable question posed by Margaret.

"To the allotment. I forgot to do something earlier." He stood up from the sofa and rushed out of the house, before any further cross-examination could follow. Having stored up the contents of several cups of tea consumed that evening, the pressure on his bladder was acute, a condition not assisted by his nervousness. The fifteen minute journey to the allotments was sheer torture, and the walk was more a twisting lurch from side to side, his buttock muscles firmly clenched to avoid an accident.

The thin crescent of a moon on the wane just about provided sufficient light for him to see his way to the metal gate of the allotments. To his surprise, the gate was open. As he made his way gingerly along the path, heading for his plot, he saw a figure stumbling towards him out of the darkness, a mere outline without any discernible identity. Struggling to resist the impulse to freeze - he was an officer of the law after all - he cautiously continued, although the resultant adrenalin surge almost did for his bladder. As the figure loomed closer in to his field of vision, he recognised the features. They both stopped.

"Hugo, whatever are you doing here at this time?"

"Jusht attending to shome matters," came the slurred retort of a manifestly worse for wear Hugo Wivelsfield. "What ish you up to. Shomeshing shameful, if you ashk me. Hic."

Nigel decided that honesty was the best policy, banking that in the state he was in, there was every chance that Hugo would neither remember anything nor cause a fuss the next day. "Vital job, Hugo I'm about to piss on my compost heap. Help the process along."

"Hic. You're shurely taking the pish," said Hugo, an unexpectedly entertaining riposte given his inebriated condition.

"No I'm not. In point of fact, I'm actually giving the piss. It's quite the done thing, and scientifically based. Urine is rich in nitrogen but it has to be men's not women's. Women's is too acidic. According to some website I looked at, one person can provide enough pee to fertilize 6,300 tomato plants a year. That yields 2.4 tons of tomatoes. Apparently farmers in Nepal have been urinating on their crops for centuries."

"Fashinating, Nige. Shpose it's safer than shcaling the Himalayas. Musht go now. Musht get home." Hugo shuffled off towards the exit to the allotment, lurching from side to side, his presence having answered the mystery as to why the gate was open at this time of night.

More by luck than any positive feat on his part, Nigel reached his plot without an accident and after checking that there was no-one else in sight, ejected the contents of his bladder over the compost heap. Relieved of his burden, he replaced the plastic covering, left the allotments after locking the gate and returned home.

Margaret was asleep in the bed. "Everything alright, dear," she murmured by instinct, barely stirring. Nigel's nocturnal comings and goings were not unusual.

"Fine. Mission accomplished. Night night."

\*\*\*\*\*\*\*\*\*\*\*\*\*\*\*


The results of his nocturnal endeavour materialised sometime later, although in truth Nigel would never know for sure if the natural liquid additive had made the slightest difference. Certainly there was a strange odour pervading the greenhouse, emerging to hang in the air on windless days, but he could never discern whether the source of this was his organically fertilised compost or the distinctive green-leaved greenhouse-veiled plants in the middle of his patch.

"That's ever such an exquisite plant by your left boot, Nigel," boomed an all too inimitable voice.

Trust Daphne to spot the one plant leaf peeking out from under the gap in the makeshift greenhouse. She was such an interfering cow. Nothing escaped her attentive eagle eye. Everybody's business was her business. "Yes, the coriander is doing well this year. Must be the effect of my special compost," he said, smiling knowingly to himself.

"Never seen coriander with leaves that shape?"

"It's a special variety. Vietnamese coriander. Essential ingredient for some dishes, and very therapeutic."

"Vietnamese coriander?" she exclaimed, her resounding voice carrying over the surrounding plots.

Back in the day, Concorde breaking the sound barrier could hardly have sounded any louder, he thought. "Indeed. Vietnamese coriander. Quite an enigma of a plant."

"An enigma indeed, but with variations," came another voice, most definitely not Daphne's as it was undoubtedly male.

Nigel looked over Daphne's shoulder as Clive wandered up, his attention presumably aroused by the percussive impact of Daphne's very own sonic boom.

"Clive, we don't see you here very often these days," Nigel said, relieved by the potential distraction from any further questions provided by Clive's advent.

"Clive, how nice to see you. We *are* honoured with your attendance," came the intervention from Daphne, the sarcasm all too apparent, her grin spoiled by the yellow-stained teeth seemingly trying to break free from her mouth. "Is Stacey not with you?"

"No. She has something else on. Did you see the match last night, Nigel? Weren't Barcelona fantastic?"

Nigel caught on at once that Clive didn't want to engage with Daphne, and decided to help him out. "Yes, I watched the match. Wonderful, Arsenal were completely outclassed." He felt that the last thing Daphne would want was to wait for a discussion on European football to run its course while she stood by like a wallflower, totally ignored.

"Must take Winnie home and feed the cats," she said, after an awkward pause, and marched off.

"Thanks for that," said Nigel. "I don't see that I should have to account for my comings and goings, let alone those of my wife.'"

"I couldn't agree more. She's quite out of order. The toerag."

There was a momentary break in their conversation, as if they were each considering what to say next. The gap was filled by Clive.

"Err, about your plants, the Vietnamese coriander."

"Truly there is a variety of Vietnamese coriander."

"I know there is. But the leaf shape is wrong, and ipso factor your crop is not Vietnamese coriander. It's something else. Handsome weed, wouldn't you say. Bit dodgy for a police officer to grow such stuff, isn't it? You're asking for trouble."

"I don't know what you mean?" Nigel blurted out, his blustering attempt to express ignorance sounding less than convincing, even to himself.

"I once represented a client in court charged with growing the stuff in his house. It was actually a rented house. He had intercepted the electricity supply to the meter, so it didn't show the full use of electricity used to keep the rooms heated. A neighbour complained about the strange smell coming down her chimney."

"What was the outcome?"

"Oh, he pleaded guilty on my advice. Plea mitigation. He was still committed to prison though."

"You must deal with some weird and wonderful cases, Clive?"

"One certainly learns a lot about life. I've dabbled a fair bit in drugs."

"Really? Are you sure you want to tell me that? I am a police officer, remember?"

They both laughed. "No, you misunderstand. Mischievously no doubt. I've handled the odd drugs case in my time. You learn all the ins and outs. Brown, white, that sort of thing. How the drug-dealing process works. Makes for an interesting time."

"Well, alright. No need to tell me any more." Nigel looked at his watch. "iI's not that late. Fancy a quick one, before we go home to our better halves? Shall we repair to the Flounder and Ferret? My shout."

Clive glanced in turn at his watch. "Sure, why not. You really ought to destroy your crop, you know. Don't worry, I won't grass on you, to coin a phrase, but do be careful with Daphne Littlehampton. You know what she's like."

"Of course you won't say anything about this," said Nigel, waving his hand in the direction of the green leaved plants, "just as I'll keep shtum about the boy I saw you with in your car a couple of weeks back."

"I don't know anything…I…that was my son," stammered Clive.

"I believe your son is somewhat older than that callow youth. I innocently enquired about your children with your wife. Don't worry, I was discreet. She won't suspect anything. Do we understand each other?" said Nigel, with just a hint of understated threat in his question.

"Pro bono publico, as we lawyers say. I believe we do," Nigel responded, and shook the proffered hand.

They both packed away their gardening tools, changed out of their mud-caked allotment footwear, and wandered off to the pub.

## Clive's courgettes

It was something of an inevitability waiting to happen, he had always thought. And now it had. In many ways, the most surprising thing was that he had got away undetected for such a long time. No doubt if Stacey had not been distracted elsewhere - that much was obvious from the withering of her untended cucumbers - she would have realised something was amiss far sooner.

It happened one night as he returned home. For once a client meeting had been cancelled and he had left the office early and gone direct to the allotment, conscious of the need to check on the courgettes now that summer was almost over, not that it had begun that year. Stacey was nowhere to be seen. Some of the courgettes had turned yellow and started to rot, not really surprising in view of their inattention. He had developed a reluctance to go down to the allotment, preferring to avoid the place and the motley bunch of people for whom it appeared to be the centre of their existence. He picked a selection of the firmer dark-green ones and set off for the exit, only to find Nigel and Daphne in a lively exchange in the middle of the path.

Nigel was clearly on the receiving end of one of Daphne's diatribes and Clive made the decision to intervene in an effort to somehow blunt the verbal assault. By butting in and switching the topic to that week's football, he was spared a lengthy exposure to her as she had not the faintest interest and left to feed her cats. He continued the chat with Nigel, who unsurprisingly was grateful for being rescued, although their conversation took an unexpected course.

Funny how stuff can emerge out of nowhere, and secrets escape their bonds of restraint. The ensuing quick one at the Flounder and Ferret had morphed into two, or was it three, and it was some considerably later hour that he got into the car and drove home.

He drew up in the car outside his house. It was already dusk and all of a sudden, the hall light was turned on. As he watched, he saw the silhouettes of two figures through the frosted glass panel of the front door merge into one. Clive froze, stunned at the brazenness of what was too obviously going on, and in his own home at that. But why was he surprised, he asked himself. Stacey devoted more and more time to the allotment, or so she told him, and she seemed distracted and completely worn out when he returned from work in the evening.

Of course, he suspected that there was someone else in her life. Daphne Littlehampton had implied as much in a snide aside to him at the allotment AGM a few weeks ago. Although Daphne had hedged her words, the import had been all too clear. There was something going on between his wife and Hugo Wivelsfield, the man who worked one of the nearby allotment plots to theirs.

****************

He and Stacey had been married for over twenty years. God knows how, he wondered. Clive had grown up in a small Home Counties town in the 1960s. Short in stature bookish and shy by nature, he had been bullied at his local grammar school. And the other things, in the changing room of the swimming pool, involving the games master. That was the start of the path. University followed, red-brick Russell Group rather than Oxbridge, and a second-class degree in law. He knew he had the potential to obtain a first, but was too lazy to put in the necessary hours.

Now his hair had receded and turned grey with the passing years, but prior to that he had a full head of sleek brown hair. Although no-one would have described him as good looking, he was eminently presentable and had developed a certain bearing as he gained more professional experience in the courts.

Before meeting Stacey, he had always found it difficult to sustain a relationship. He had been out with a few women, but never felt any urge to go beyond the mild petting stages. He found it easy to admit to himself, although rarely to others, that his natural lethargy did not help. There never felt any kind of drive to chase after women, unlike many of his fellow students at law school or male work colleagues in the legal practice.

Whilst they appeared fuelled by an unquenchable desire to make a fresh conquest from amongst the new student intake or latest interns, he lacked any similar feeling or urge. Women seemed to hold no appeal to him. He devoted his energies, such as they were, to the intricacies of the law. And he most definitely never told any of his work colleagues about the other aspect of his life.

Once established in the law practice in his mid-twenties, his life revolved around the office and necessary court appearances, He generally shunned the dinners and local Law Society activities. He simply couldn't be bothered with legal small talk, the indignant outrage at some highhanded courtroom injustice at the hands of a fusty and crusty judge, or the inveterate bragging about some inconsequential legal success.

Clive had at some stage joined the local Rotary club, largely because all the other solicitors in the practice were members and there was some pressure to conform and join the club, but he disassociated himself from most of the activities. This was less to do with any distaste for the rituals, tedious though he found them, but more that he couldn't really be bothered. The senior partner had remarked on his lack of get-up-and-go – a benignly slothful disposition as he had put it - at one of their periodic reviews of his casework.

At the insistence of the senior partner, he had attended a reception for the Fashion Week that his firm was sponsoring. It was there that he had met Stacey, who had been the most talked about model at the week's events, as much for her nocturnal deeds as for the fashion displays.

Quite out of nowhere, she had latched on to him at the reception. He had been standing at the drinks table on his own, wondering why he had come and on the verge of going home; suddenly she was standing next to him, her unexpected presence manifesting itself initially by the musky scent of her perfume.

"I see you have a large one", had been her opening remark.

He had felt the full flush of his face reddening, as he attempted to respond. "No, I...I..."

"I would love a large one", she added, bewitchingly fluttering her eyelashes and holding firm eye contact, as she proffered her empty glass.

Completely out of character for him, he had felt an instant attraction to her and a stirring of something deep down he had not experienced before. She was absolutely stunning, and fully aware of it, with sparkling emerald green eyes and shoulder length lustrous golden blonde hair. Her alluring fragrance felt as if it was reaching out to embrace him, and to envelope him in a warm cocoon, detaching him from the general hubbub of the reception which had now receded into the background.

He had readily agreed to her suggestion that they leave the reception, which in any event he felt no part of, and go for something to eat. Their conversation flowed over the expensive food at a pretentious restaurant, no doubt desperately seeking the award of a Michelin star. He had some delicate pasta dish, minimalist portion centred in the well of a ginormous white plate; she had nibbled at a salad. To his utter amazement when he later thought back over the evening's events, he had ended up back at her flat, and stayed the night. And what a night! So, this was what passionate sex with a woman was all about.

Six months later, in what at the time had felt the natural order of events, they had married and settled down together. His fellow legal practitioners had treated him with a new found respect, which he knew masked their envy, as she accompanied him round the circuit of legal dinners and functions he now found the urge to attend. He would be more than aware of the glances as Stacey floated on his arm through the Ascot, Goodwood and Henley of the social calendar of the local legal establishment, to which had developed an attachment, previously lacking. That attachment was Stacey.

Dinner parties, foreign exotic holidays, two children and parental bereavements, had come and gone over the years of their marriage, as they had settled into a life of routine bordering on monotonous tedium. Stacey seemed to spend most of her days on the allotment they had managed to acquire at some stage in their voyage through everyday existence into early middle age. Clive had long since retrenched into his earlier life of languor and indolence, spending most weekdays buried in legal casework, evenings when at home slumped on the sofa watching football matches on the multitude of satellite channels, and weekends skimming through the thicket of newspapers and supplements. The burgeoning pile of discarded inserts and advertising flyers sat glaringly on the kitchen top for weeks, until Stacey eventually tidied up, pointing out sharply the lack of action on his part.

Physicality with Stacey had long since faded from the early period of their relationship. They had discussed the lack of mutual desire in an offhand manner, much as they discussed changing their gas or broadband provider. Except that with a utility, there were always a number of alternative providers of the service. On further reflection, he once mused, perhaps they are more similar than would appear to be the case on first thought. There we have it, he ruminated, his lawyerly prose kicking in.

"Do you still fancy me as much as you did when we first met?" Stacey had enquired on one of their wedding anniversaries over a three-course meal in a two Michelin star restaurant. He had booked this – or rather his secretary had – a couple of weeks previously. Having forgotten the previous year's occasion, and been severely castigated, he felt under the burden of obligation to make amends this time.

"Of course I do," he replied instinctively. "Why do you need to ask?"

"Well...it's just that..." The remainder of the sentence was left unsaid, but they both were highly conscious of the words that were missing.

"How was your fish?" he asked, aware that a pause in their conversation was not commensurate with the occasion.

She murmured some rote comment in response. Her original question was entirely valid, but did he have a valid answer? Did he fancy her as much as when they had first met? The absence of regular sex between them probably indicated the point they had reached in their lives far clearer than any conversation could convey. He still regarded Stacey as a soulmate, a life partner. Was it still love, he wondered to himself? After a fashion, he supposed. But what is love? His thoughts were interrupted by the realisation that Stacey had said something.

"Sorry, what did you say?"

"I asked you whether you enjoyed your venison?"

"Yes, it was fine. Done on the outside but still pink inside. Just right."

He knew that Stacey still caused heads to turn, and in mid-forties retained the natural glamour she possessed when they had first got together. At the restaurant, as they made their way to the allotted table, he was conscious of glances in her direction as she sashayed in front of him through the crowded room. Even he had noticed that Stacey had glammed up, her hair flowing, her gold necklace and earrings glowing, and her emerald green dress with plunging neckline wowing all around her.

He had never said anything to Stacey about the other, as he termed it. He had once been on the brink of revealing all, but the moment had passed by the time he had summoned up the courage. So he said nothing, and continued with the normality of his everyday customs and practices, a legal term from the safe world of employment law if ever there was one. Appearances can be so deceptive, he thought to himself.

After their children had fled the homely nest, the lack of physicality with Stacey had meant that their relationship had weakened. He could explain it to himself, but felt inhibited in raising the issue with her. He knew he was no longer the ardent soulmate and life partner she had first married, but felt helpless to do anything to change matters, or whether he even wanted to.

The allotment no longer offered the escape it once had, with the exception of the courgettes which offered some mild appeal and required minimal upkeep. He found the other allotment holders an odd assortment. Misshapen, very much like the products of his labours with the vegetables in the early stages of allotment familiarisation. As he grew more and more bored with the duties and responsibilities of allotment life, he became ever more slothful at the plot. Although he had willingly joined in at the start, he had long ceased to participate in the work days, when all allotment holders were expected to join together for some communal chore or other.

One hot summer Sunday afternoon, having wandered down to inspect the state of play of his courgettes, he had sat down on the wobbly metal chair that they had found somewhere else and opened the beer he had brought from the house. Bottle in hand, he surveyed the group at the far end of the allotment ground, busy at work on some activity whose purpose was not readily apparent. As the group dispersed and some walked past where he was sitting, he caught the murmur of their voices and the all too obvious glances in his direction.

The mutterings. There were always mutterings on the allotments. He sensed they were usually aimed at him, snide utterings and mutterings, mumblings and grumblings. Well, if that was what they wanted he could do without it, and his visits to the allotment became even fewer and far between.

His only continuing item of interest – and a mild one at that - was the courgettes. He was intrigued on his infrequent visits by the way in which the delicate yellow flowers perched on the end of slender green tubes of flesh, sometimes appearing from nowhere overnight. A gardening column in one of the weekend glossy supplements had referred in some detail to the intricate sex life of the courgette, seemingly a world away from his own with Stacey. The apparent happenstance of fertilisation, and whether a form developed and grew. Now was he thinking of the human or the vegetable condition?

He was not the only allotment holder to observe a connection between the two. The man who held a nearby plot, a fairly recent arrival, had stopped on the bordering path to cast his eye over the crop on their allotment. At least, that was what Clive had surmised at the time.

"Interesting crop of courgettes you have there," said the man, although his gaze seemed to be over Clive's shoulder. "I'm a newcomer here, to allotment activity. We haven't introduced ourselves. I'm Hugo. Hugo Wivelsfield"

"I'm Clive. Clive Portslade. And this is my wife, Stacey." Clive turned round and saw Stacey looking up at the subject who had prompted this bout of introductions.

"That is an especially shapely specimen you have there," the man he now knew as Hugo continued, "and all over its neighbour. A veritable Kama Sutra of entanglement."

Stacey giggled irrepressibly but he thought little of it. The phrase used by Hugo had lodged in his brain, Clive thinking at the time that this was a highly forward turn of phrase for a first encounter. Kama Sutra entanglement might aptly describe the entwining of the courgette stems, but not the by now stage and state of his relationship with Stacey.

He had found other substitutes – or were they alternatives - for the absence of physicality with Stacey, and wondered whether she had done likewise. Well, not quite likewise. In the subsequent weeks, she started to put on makeup, and studiously examine her appearance, before leaving to go round to the allotment. While the vegetables would be unlikely to give her a passing glance, that could not be said for Hugo Wivelsfield. Even Clive could hardly fail to be aware of the body language which passed between them in the weeks following their initial encounter.

At the buffet following the most recent AGM of the allotment-holders, that interfering busybody Daphne Littlehampton had sidled up to him as he moved away from the drinks table, glass in hand.

"Despite your lack of attention, your courgettes seem to be flourishing and extending themselves very generously" she simpered, and paused. "Just like your wife."

And with that, she had glided away, no doubt to spread some further morsel of gossip from the allotments to anyone who would listen, not that you had any choice once she had apprehended you, he thought. Daphne did not take any prisoners.

It had been the first annual meeting Clive had attended for some years. They were long winded, bureaucratic affairs, with tiresome people full of allotment business. Vegetables obsessed by vegetables, he thought to himself. Unusually that particular AGM had for once been out of the ordinary. The row that had blown up as a result of a kerfuffle about a pumpkin. Who would have believed it? Still, it centred on Hugo Wivelsfield, whom he considered had the manner of a fraud ever since their first exchange. He had met a few over the years in the courts and he considered himself well-studied in being able to pick out those who were not the sea-green incorruptibles they purported to be.

\*\*\*\*\*\*\*\*\*\*\*\*\*\*\*

His thoughts returned to the present. He opened the car door and got out, walking slowly but deliberately up the path to the front door, his shoes crunching loudly in the gravel. He inserted his key in the lock and paused momentarily before opening the door and entering. Stacey was still in the embrace he had seen from the car, but she suddenly saw him and broke away from the man she had been kissing. Clive immediately recognised the man who had turned round, seemingly startled. Unsurprisingly, it was that preening creep

Hugo from the allotment. He calmly told him to leave, and Hugo departed without saying a word, not that there was much he could say.

Clive looked at Stacey, thinking how to broach what he had decided to say.

"I think we had better sit down in the lounge and talk", and with that he turned his back on Stacey and walked towards the door into the lounge.

Once inside, he stood with his back to the room, staring out through the patio doors into the garden.

Conscious of her entry into the room, he turned round to face her.

"I...I...I...I'm sorry," she rather lamely started to say, "it won't happen again."

"..oh that. Your affair with that drip Hugo? I've known about that for months."

"You…you knew?" Stacey said, stumbling over the words in what was clearly complete disbelief.

"Yes of course."

"Oh darling, I didn't mean to hurt you."

"Yes, well, bit late for that."

"I never would have wanted to hurt you. But we have drifted apart, haven't we?"

"Please sit down."

"I…I…I don't know what to say. It won't happen again. Are you very angry with me?"

"Sit down, please. Listen to me for a minute. There is something I need to tell you."

Stacey sat down. Her state of anxiety was impossible to hide.

"I've also not been straight with you," he said, thinking as he said it that it was a completely inappropriate phrase in view of what he was about to confess.

"I've also been having an affair", he declared. "That's why I have been away overnight so much recently".

"What!! You?? I…I…I…don't know what to say", she responded shakily, after a momentary pause.

Although she was obviously shocked, Clive thought he detected an element of relief in her voice.

"Who is she?" Stacey continued, regaining some of her normal composure. "Someone at work? What's her name?"

"No,". Now was the moment, the moment he had been readying himself for a long time.

"He. He's called Toby"

"Oh. Oh, I see," she exclaimed, demonstrably shocked. "Do I know this man?"

"No." He paused. "Not part of our circle. Younger"

"Mm. How much younger?"

"Well...quite a bit."

"Well then. 35, 30?"

"Nooo."

"Younger?"

"Y...yes"

"How much younger?"

"Erm..."

"I'm waiting," she demanded.

"Erm, 15 actually."

"Clive. How could you?" she wailed, and bent over. After a moment, she sat up and recovered her composure, looking beseechingly at him.

"Whilst we are at it, there is something I need to tell you," she carried on, haltingly." I've never told you before, nor anyone for that matter. Please sit down with me."

He sat down. She paused, unsure whether to carry on but then plunged in. "When I was in my early teens, I had issues with my father."

"Oh, what kind of issues?" he enquired, quietly.

"Err, he…he… physically abused me.," she just about managed to get out.

"He hit you?"

"Yes, but rather more than that. Much more."

"You mean…"

"Yes," she replied, sobbing her heart out.

Maybe it was the sight of her tears, maybe the relief of revealing his secret life, but suddenly it all welled up inside and he burst out crying uncontrollably. They fell into each other's arms and embraced.

For all their married life, they had continued to share the same king-sized bed, albeit with a divide the width of an ocean between them, but tonight they lay close together for once, some of the long abandoned shared intimacy returning.

He had drifted off, when he was suddenly awakened by the doorbell and a loud hammering at the front door. Stacey groaned and told him to see who was there at this hour of the night. Half asleep, he put on his silk dressing gown she had bought him for some long-forgotten occasion, and went downstairs with some trepidation.

Staring through the peephole, he realised it was Nigel, so he unlocked and opened the door.

Nigel was hopping from one leg to the other, completely stressed out, that much was apparent.

"Thank goodness you were awake," Nigel cried, "I didn't know who to call. Down at the allotment. You need to come. I don't know what to do, in spite of all my years in he force."

"At this time of night? Why, what's up?", Clive enquired blearily.

"It's Daphne."

"Oh, her. What about her?

"I saw a light flickering from her shed, on the allotment."

"I'm sure there's an explanation. There's supposedly a blood moon tonight. Maybe she decided to wander down to have a look at the night sky away from all the street lights," Clive said.

"The why is neither here or there. It's the what."

"What is ...the what?" Clive started, and then realised it didn't make much sense.

"The what is she is slumped with her eyes wide open."

"Perhaps she has had one drink too many, Daphne is partial to one too many. What's the problem? Why are you disturbing me at this time of night?"

"The problem is she's dead," Nigel yelled, "and there's an open bottle of paraquat on the floor of the shed."

"It can't be. Paraquat is banned in England," expounded Clive, the knowledgeable lawyer.

"That's as may be, but there is an open bottle of the stuff. And she's dead. Stone dead."

"How do you know she's dead?"

"I'm a police officer when all said and done, and I know a dead body when I see one."

Printed in Great Britain
by Amazon